MAGIC
kitten & puppy

A Christmas
Surprise & Snowy
Wishes

Sue Bentley's books for children often include animals, fairies and wildlife. She lives in Northampton and enjoys reading, going to the cinema, relaxing by her garden pond and watching the birds feeding their babies on the lawn. At school she was always getting told off for daydreaming or staring out of the window – but she now realizes that she was storing up ideas for when she became a writer. She has met and owned many cats and dogs and each one has brought a special kind of magic to her life.

MAGIC
kitten&puppy

A Christmas Surprise & Snowy Wishes

SUE BENTLEY

Illustrated by Angela Swan

PUFFIN

AM1883

PUFFIN BOOKS

Published by the Penguin Group
Penguin Books Ltd, 80 Strand, London WC2R ORL, England
Penguin Group (USA) Inc., 375 Hudson Street, New York, New York 10014, USA
Penguin Group (Canada), 90 Eglinton Avenue East, Suite 700, Toronto, Ontario, Canada M4P 2Y3
(a division of Pearson Penguin Canada Inc.)
Penguin Ireland, 25 St Stephen's Green, Dublin 2, Ireland (a division of Penguin Books Ltd)
Penguin Group (Australia), 250 Camberwell Road, Camberwell, Victoria 3124, Australia
(a division of Pearson Australia Group Pty Ltd)
Penguin Books India Pvt Ltd, 11 Community Centre, Panchsheel Park, New Delhi – 110 017, India
Penguin Group (NZ), 67 Apollo Drive, Rosedale, Auckland 0632, New Zealand
(a division of Pearson New Zealand Ltd)
Penguin Books (South Africa) (Pty) Ltd, 24 Sturdee Avenue, Rosebank, Johannesburg 2196, South Africa

Penguin Books Ltd, Registered Offices: 80 Strand, London WC2R ORL, England

puffinbooks.com

Magic Kitten: A Christmas Surprise first published 2007
Magic Puppy: Snowy Wishes first published 2008
First published in one volume 2011
001 – 10 9 8 7 6 5 4 3 2 1

Text copyright © Sue Bentley, 2007, 2008
Illustrations copyright © Angela Swan, 2007, 2008
All rights reserved

The moral right of the author and illustrator has been asserted

Set in Bembo by Palimpsest Book Production Limited, Falkirk, Stirlingshire
Printed in Great Britain by Clays Ltd, St Ives plc

Except in the United States of America, this book is sold subject to the condition that it shall not,
by way of trade or otherwise, be lent, re-sold, hired out, or otherwise circulated without the publisher's
prior consent in any form of binding or cover other than that in which it is published and without
a similar condition including this condition being imposed on the subsequent purchaser

British Library Cataloguing in Publication Data
A CIP catalogue record for this book is available from the British Library

ISBN: 978-0-141-34073-9

www.greenpenguin.co.uk

MIX
Paper from
responsible sources
FSC
www.fsc.org   FSC™ C018179

Penguin Books is committed to a sustainable
future for our business, our readers and our
planet. This book is made from paper certified
by the Forest Stewardship Council.

To Tibby, my fondly remembered marmalade sweetie

To Teddy – tiny dog with a big heart

MAGIC kitten

A Christmas Surprise

MISSING!

Flame

Have you seen this kitten?

Flame is a magic kitten of royal blood, missing from his own world.
His uncle, Ebony, is very keen that he is found quickly.
Flame may be hard to spot as he often appears in a
variety of fluffy kitten colours but you can recognize him
by his big emerald eyes and whiskers that crackle with magic!

He is believed to be looking for a young friend to take care of him.

Could it be you?

If you find this very special kitten please let Ebony,
ruler of the Lion Throne, know.

Prologue

Dust swirled round the young white lion's paws as he bounded through the dry valley. Flame knew he shouldn't risk being out in the open. But maybe this time it would be safe.

Suddenly, a terrifying roar rang out and an enormous black adult lion burst out from behind some thorn trees and bounded towards him.

'Ebony!'

Flame leapt into a clump of tall grass. A bright white flash filled the air and where he had once stood, now crouched a tiny, snowy-white kitten with a fluffy tail.

Flame's heart thudded in his tiny chest as he edged slowly backwards to where the grass grew more thickly. His Uncle Ebony was very close. He hoped this disguise would protect him.

The stems to one side of Flame parted with a rustle and a big dark shape pushed towards him. Flame tensed ready to fight, his emerald eyes sparking with anger and fear.

'Stay there, Prince Flame. I will protect you,' growled a deep but gentle voice.

Flame gave a faint mew of relief, as an old grey lion peered down at him. 'Cirrus. I am glad to see you again. I had hoped that by now, Ebony would be ready to give back the throne he stole from me.'

Cirrus shook his head gravely. 'That will never happen. Your uncle is determined to rule in your place and sends many spies to search for you and kill you. It is not safe for you to be here. Use this disguise and go back to the other world to hide.'

The tiny kitten bared his sharp teeth as he looked up into Cirrus's tired old face. 'I wish I could fight him now!'

Cirrus's eyes flickered with affection. He reached out a huge paw and gently patted Flame's tiny fluffy white head.

'Bravely said, but now is not the time. Return when you are strong and wise.'

Suddenly another mighty roar rang out. The ground shook as huge paws thundered into the tall grass and then came the cracking of crushed stems.

'You cannot hide from me!' roared Ebony's harsh cruel voice.

'Save yourself, Flame! Go quickly!' Cirrus urged.

Sparks glowed in the tiny kitten's silky white fur. Flame mewed softly as he felt the power building inside him. He felt himself falling. Falling . . .

★ Chapter ★
ONE

'I really hope it's going to be a white Christmas!' Molly Paget said, peering hopefully out of the landing window. She sighed as raindrops snaked down the glass and blurred her view of the street outside. 'Oh, well. There's still a week to go.'

Molly jumped down the stairs two at a time and went into the kitchen where a delicious spicy smell filled the air. Her mum was just fetching a tray of mince pies out of the oven.

Mrs Paget looked up and smiled. 'I heard you clumping down the stairs. What's the hurry?'

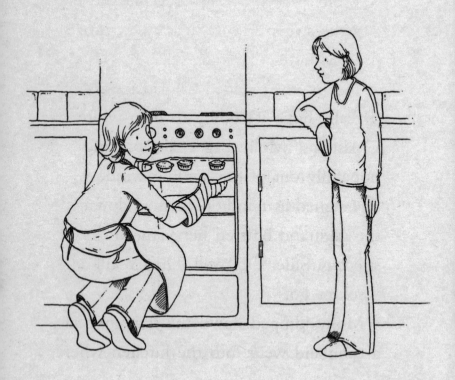

Molly grinned. 'There isn't one. I'm just feeling in a good mood. Can I have one of those pies?'

Her mum nodded. 'Course you can. Take one of those on the plate, they're cooler.'

Molly picked up a mince pie and bit into the sweet crumbly pastry. 'Mmm, yummy. Tastes Christmassy!'

Her mum smiled. 'I'm glad it passes the Molly test!'

'When are Gran and Gramps arriving?' Molly asked, munching.

Her grandparents lived near the coast. She hadn't seen them since the summer holidays, but they were going to spend Christmas at Molly's house. Molly's eyebrows dipped in a small frown as she remembered how during the last visit to her grandparents' house, she had had to take her shoes off before going into the sitting room. Everyone always sat at the table to eat and no one was allowed to watch TV in the daytime. Molly hoped Gran would be less strict this Christmas.

'They'll be here the day before Christmas Eve,' her mum said, wiping her hands on her apron. 'I've still got puddings to make, a cake to ice and heaps of presents to buy. And we haven't even made a start on clearing out the spare bedroom.' A worried look crossed her face. 'Your gran's lovely, but she has very high standards.'

Tell me about it, Molly thought. 'I'll help you. I'm brilliant at clearing up and stuff,' she said brightly.

'It's nice of you to offer, but Molly and the word "help" can sometimes spell trouble!' Mrs Paget said wryly, ruffling her daughter's blonde hair. 'I'll get your dad to give me a hand with the bedroom. It's his parents who are staying, after all.'

'Did I hear my name mentioned?' Mr Paget said, coming into the kitchen. His hair was speckled with dust and there were cobwebs sticking to his blue jumper. He quickly washed his hands before helping himself to a mince pie.

'Da–ad! You've got yucky stuff all over you,' Molly said, laughing. She reached up to pick off a cobweb.

'Have I? I didn't notice,' Mr Paget said around a mouthful of pie. 'I've just been in the attic. I had to move a mountain of old rubbish to get to the Christmas tree and decorations. Anyway, I found them in the end. They're in the sitting room.'

'Brilliant!' Molly said excitedly, already speeding out of the kitchen. 'I'm going to put the tree up right now!'

'Slow down a bit, Molly!' her mum called after her.

But Molly had already gone. Mr Paget shook his head slowly. 'Molly's only got two speeds. Fast and faster!' he said as he followed his daughter.

By the time her dad came into the sitting room, Molly had her arms full of folded, green spiky branches. 'There's an awful lot of tree,' she said peering into the long box. 'I don't remember it being so huge.'

Mr Paget laughed. 'Well it can't have grown since last year, can it, you muppet? I'll fetch the step-ladder.'

'That's a job well done!' Mr Paget said an hour later.

Molly looked up at the Christmas

tree, which almost touched the sitting-
room ceiling. 'It's dead impressive. I
can't wait to decorate it!' She fished
about in another cardboard box and
produced some tissue-wrapped packages.
Unwrapping one of them, she looked
closely at the blue glass bauble. 'Isn't
this lovely? It's got silver-frosted
snowflake patterns all over it,' she said
delightedly. 'Have we got any more
like this?'

Her dad nodded. 'There are lots of
them. I remember them hanging on
our Christmas tree when I was little.'

'Really? They must be ancient then,'
Molly said.

'Cheeky!' Mr Paget said, grinning,
giving her a playful nudge in the arm.
'I'd forgotten we had those baubles. Be

very careful with them, won't you?'

'I will,' Molly promised, unpacking the precious baubles very gently.

Mr Paget peered into the empty cardboard box. 'That's funny. I thought the tinsel and other stuff was in there too. Maybe it's in the garage. I'll go and have a look.'

Molly frowned. She knew that her dad couldn't resist tidying up when he was looking for things. He was bound to be ages. 'Aw, do you have to do it now, Dad?'

Mr Paget grinned at the look on her face. 'Impatient to get going, aren't you? Why don't you make a start on the bottom branches? But you'd better wait for me to come back before you do the ones higher up.'

'OK!' Molly said, already tearing open a packet of little green plastic hooks.

As soon as he'd gone she began hanging baubles on the tree. Soon, the bottom branches were finished. Molly stood back to admire the

way the blue, red and gold glass
gleamed prettily against the dark
green.

Her dad still hadn't come back.
Molly looked longingly up at the
higher branches. She shifted her feet
impatiently. 'Come on, Dad, you
slowcoach,' she grumbled. She hesitated
for a moment longer and then
dragged the step-ladder closer to
the tree.

He was bound to be back in a
minute. She'd just start doing a few
more branches. Climbing halfway up
the ladder, she began fixing baubles to
the branches that were within easy
reach.

This is easy, she thought, *I don't know
what Dad was worrying about.*

She climbed higher to hang more decorations. At this rate, she'd soon have the whole tree finished. At the top of the ladder, Molly leaned out further to try and reach a branch near the top of the tree that would look perfect with the bauble she was holding.

And then she felt the ladder wobble.

'Oops!' Throwing out her arms, Molly tried to grab something to steady herself, but her fingers closed on thin air. She lost her balance and banged against the tree. It shook wildly and decorations began pinging off in all directions.

Molly heard the precious baubles smash into tiny pieces as they hit the carpet. 'Oh, no!' she wailed.

She looked down as she swayed sideways and then everything seemed to happen at once. The ladder and tree both tipped sideways and started to fall to the ground.

'He-elp!' Molly croaked, tensing her whole body for the painful bruising thud as she hit the carpet.

Suddenly, the room filled with a dazzling white flash and a shower of silver sparks. Molly felt a strange warm tingling sensation down her spine as she fell. The air whistled past her ears. There was a sudden jolt, but no hard landing.

To her complete shock, Molly was hovering in mid-air half a metre above the carpet. Swirling all around her was

a snowstorm of brightly sparkling glitter!

She gasped as she felt herself turning and then drifting gently down to the carpet where she landed on her behind with barely a bump. The sparkling glitter fizzled like a firework and then disappeared.

Molly sat up shakily and looked around.

The ladder was upright and the tree was straight and tall once again. The delicate glass baubles were all unbroken and hanging back in place on the branches.

'But . . . I heard them smash! I don't get it . . .' Molly said to herself. What had just happened? She felt like pinching herself to see if she was dreaming.

'I hope you are not hurt?' mewed a strange little voice.

Molly almost jumped out of her skin. 'Who said that?' She twisted round, her eyes searching the room.

Crouching beneath the Christmas tree, Molly saw a tiny fluffy snow-white kitten. Its silky fur seemed to glitter with a thousand tiny, diamond-bright sparkles and it had the biggest emerald eyes she had ever seen.

★ Chapter ★
TWO

Molly's eyes widened. She must be
more confused and shaken up by her
fall than she'd thought. She'd just
imagined that the kitten had spoken
to her!

She looked at the kitten again and
now its silky white fur and bushy tail
looked normal. Perhaps it had wandered
in when her dad left the door open on

his way to the garage. 'Hello. Where've you come from?' she said, kneeling up and reaching a hand towards it.

'I come from far away,' the kitten mewed. 'When I saw you fall I used my magic to save you. I am sorry if I startled you.'

Molly gasped and pulled her hand back as if she had been burned. 'You . . . you can talk!' she stammered.

The kitten blinked up at her with wide green eyes. Despite its tiny size, it didn't seem to be too afraid of her. 'Yes. My name is Prince Flame. What is yours?'

'Molly. Molly Paget,' Molly said. Her mind was still whirling and she couldn't seem to take this all in. But she didn't want to scare this amazing kitten away,

so she sat back on her heels and tried
to stay as small as possible. 'Um . . . I
don't know how you did it, but thanks
for helping me. I could have hurt
myself badly.'

'You are welcome,' Flame purred and
his tiny kitten face took on a serious
look. 'Can you help me, Molly? I need
somewhere to hide.'

'Why do you need to do that?'
Molly asked.

Flame's emerald eyes lit up with
anger. 'I am heir to the Lion Throne.
My uncle Ebony has stolen it and
rules in my place. He wants to keep
my throne, so he sends his spies to
find me.'

'*Lion* Throne?' Molly said doubtfully,
looking at the tiny kitten in front
of her.

Flame didn't answer. He backed
away from the Christmas tree and
before Molly knew what was
happening she was blinded by another
bright silver flash. For a moment she
couldn't see anything. But when her
sight cleared, the kitten had gone and
in its place a magnificent young white

lion stood proudly on the carpet.

Molly gasped, scrambling backwards on her hands and knees. 'Flame?'

'Yes, it is me, Molly,' Flame replied in a deep velvety roar.

Molly gulped, just getting used to the great majestic lion, when there was a final flash of dazzling light and Flame reappeared as a silky white kitten.

'Wow! I believe you,' she whispered. 'That's a cool disguise. No one would ever know you're a prince!'

Flame pricked his tiny ears and started to tremble. 'My uncle's spies will recognize me if they find me. Will you hide me, please?'

Molly reached out and stroked Flame's soft little head. He was so tiny and helpless-looking. Her soft heart melted. 'Of course I will. You can live with me. It'll be great having you to cheer me up if Gran gets in one of her grumpy moods. I bet you're hungry, aren't you? Let's go and find you some food.'

Flame gave an eager little mew.

'Find who some food?' said her dad, coming into the room with a big cardboard box in his arms.

Molly jumped up at once and turned to face him. 'Dad! Something amazing has just happened. I almost fell off the ladder . . . I mean . . . er . . .' she stopped guiltily, deciding that it might be wise to skip that bit. 'I've just found the most amazing kitten and I'm going to look after him. And guess what, he's magic and he can ta–' she stopped suddenly again as Flame gave a piercing howl.

'Flame? What's wrong?' Molly said, crouching down to talk to him.

Flame blinked at her and then sat down on the rug and began calmly washing himself in silence. Molly

looked at him in puzzlement. Why
didn't he explain?

'You and your imagination, Molly
Paget! A talking kitten indeed!' Her dad
shook his head slowly. 'I don't know
where that little kitten came from,
but you'd best pop outside and see if
one of the neighbours is looking for
him!'

'No, they won't be . . .' Molly started
to say, but she saw Flame raise a tiny
paw and put it to his mouth, warning
her to keep quiet. 'I'll go check on the
neighbours,' she finished hastily. She
picked Flame up and went into the
front garden. 'What was all that about,
back there?' she asked him once they
were alone.

'I did not have time to explain

before your father came in that you cannot tell anyone my secret,' Flame mewed softly. 'You must promise, Molly.'

'Oh, no!' Molly's hands flew to her mouth. 'But I almost told Dad everything. Have I already put you in danger?'

Flame shook his head. 'No, it is all right. He did not believe you. Luckily, grown-up humans seem to find it difficult to believe in magic.'

Molly breathed a huge sigh of relief as she looked into Flame's serious little face. 'I promise I'll keep your secret from now on. Cross my heart and hope to die.'

Flame nodded, blinking at her happily.

'I guess we should go and pretend

to look for your owner. Come on,' Molly urged.

'So we'll just have to keep Flame . . .' Molly finished explaining as she faced her mum half an hour later. Flame nestled in her arms, purring contentedly.

Mrs Paget was stacking things in the dishwasher. She stood up and reached out to stroke Flame's soft little white ears. 'Oh, dear, we hadn't planned on having a kitten, especially with the grandparents coming to stay. But if you've asked all around . . .' she said uncertainly.

'Oh, I did. I went to *dozens* of houses and no one knew anything about a white kitten,' Molly fibbed. 'So − can I open a tin of tuna for Flame?'

Her mum smiled. 'Go on then. He's really gorgeous, isn't he? And I like his name. But I think that you might have to keep Flame in your bedroom while your gran's here.'

Molly frowned. 'Why? What's she got against kittens?'

Mrs Paget smiled. 'It's not just kittens, it's pets in general. She won't tolerate hairs on the furniture. As for muddy paw prints, wet fur, fleas – shall I go on?'

'Flame hasn't got fleas!' Molly exclaimed. 'Anyway, once Gran meets him I bet even she's bound to love him too. He's the cutest kitten there ever was.'

'I agree with you. But I wouldn't be too sure that your gran will,' her mum warned gently.

Molly hardly heard her. 'Come on, Flame, let's go and tell Dad that Mum says you can stay.' Flame looked up at her and gave an extra loud purr.

★ Chapter ★
THREE

'It's the last day of term, so we'll be just doing fun stuff at school instead of proper lessons,' Molly said to Flame as she pulled on her coat a couple of days later.

Flame had followed her into the hall, his fluffy white paws padding on the carpet.

'I have to hurry and catch the bus

now, so I'll see you later,' Molly said,
bending down to stroke him. 'I really
love having you living here and I wish
you could come with me, but we aren't
allowed to bring pets to school.'

'But I can come!' Flame told her
with a happy little mew. 'I will use my
magic to make myself invisible. Only
you will be able to see and hear me.'

'Really? That's *so* cool!' Molly said delightedly. 'OK then. Quick, can you get into my school bag before Mum and Dad see you and say you can't come with me?'

Flame nodded and jumped inside.

It was a short bus ride to school. Molly put her bag on her lap, so Flame could poke out his head and look at the brightly decorated shops and the big Christmas tree in the town square. Fairy lights glinted in the trees lining the streets and more coloured lights were strung outside the big stores.

Flame's green eyes grew round with wonder. 'I have never seen so many bright lights. They are like glow-worms in long grass,' he mewed.

'It's because of Christmas,' Molly explained in a whisper. 'The shops are full of presents and stuff and special treats.'

Flame put his head on one side. 'What is Christmas?'

'Oh, I forgot. I don't suppose you have that in your world, do you?' Molly said. 'Christmas is a special time, when all the family gets together to celebrate the baby Jesus being born. We sing carols and give each other presents and eat loads of delicious food until we feel like bursting.' She grinned. 'And we pull things called crackers that go *Bang*! Dad loves the awful jokes you get in them and he always wears his silly paper hat all afternoon!'

Flame looked a bit confused. 'It

sounds very strange, but I think I will like Christmas.'

Molly smiled. She decided to buy him a really special present and put it under the tree for him to unwrap on Christmas morning.

The bus stopped outside the school. Molly got off and shouldered her bag as she walked towards the school gate. A slim, pretty girl with long blonde hair came running up. It was Shona Lamb, one of the most popular girls in Molly's class.

'Hey, Molly!'

'Hi, Shona!' Molly replied. She noticed that Shona was wearing some fabulous new boots. 'Wow! When did you get those?' she asked admiringly. The boots were like the ones Molly

wanted for Christmas, only more
expensive-looking.

Shona glanced down at her smart
boots. 'What? Oh, yesterday. I'd
forgotten about them already. But listen,
I am *so* excited! I bet you can't guess
what Mum's going to buy me for
Christmas!'

Molly pretended to think hard. 'A sports car, a trip round the world, your own private plane?' she joked.

'Very funny. You're a riot!' Shona said, rolling her eyes. 'It's a pony! I'm starting riding lessons soon. You'll be able to come over and watch me riding my very own pony!'

'Um . . . yes,' Molly murmured, imagining Shona prancing about and showing off. *Just what I'd love to do. Not!* she thought.

Shona flicked her long blonde hair over her shoulder and turned to another girl. 'Hi, Jane! You'll never guess what I'm having —'

'As if we care!' whispered a disgusted voice at Molly's side as Shona and the other girl walked away together.

Molly turned and grinned at her best friend. 'Hi, Narinder.'

Narinder Kumar had an oval face and big dark eyes. Her shiny black plait reached to her waist and her brows were drawn together in a frown. 'Sorry, but I can't stand Shona Lamb. She's so spoilt!'

'She can be a bit of a pain,' Molly agreed. 'But I don't mind her. Listen, there's the bell.'

In the classroom, Molly opened her school bag so Flame could jump out. He gave himself a shake and then began washing. Molly knew that Flame was only visible to her, but she couldn't help looking around nervously. When no one seemed to pay Flame any attention, though, she relaxed.

The teacher took the register.
Everyone answered as their names were
called. '. . . Molly Paget,' called Miss
Garret.

There was no reply.

'Molly?' Miss Garret said again.

Narinder nudged Molly. 'Miss Garret's
calling your name out.'

Molly did a double take. She had
been watching Flame leap from desk to
desk, his bushy white tail streaming out
behind him. 'Sorry! Here, Miss!' she
shouted.

'Thank you, Molly,' Miss Garret said
patiently. She finished the register and
put it away before speaking to the class.
'Now, everyone, we won't be doing any
schoolwork today. We're all going to
watch the younger children performing

their Christmas play in an hour's time,
so we've just time for a quick tidy-up.'

When Molly, Narinder and everyone
else groaned Miss Garret smiled.
'Cheer up! It won't take long. Abi and
Heather, would you tidy the
bookshelves . . .' she began giving out
jobs to all the class, '. . . and Molly and
Narinder, perhaps you could sort out
the art stuff, please?'

'OK, Miss!' Molly jumped up
helpfully.

In the storeroom, she and Narinder
tidied paper, paints and brushes. Molly
spotted a big spray can of fake snow on
a high shelf. 'Hey, look at this. It's given
me a great idea.'

'What are you going to do?' Narinder
asked.

'Wait and see!' Molly slipped the can under her school jumper.

While Narinder was putting the last few things away, Molly wandered across to the window where Flame was curled up.

'What is that? Is it something nice to eat?' the tiny kitten mewed eagerly.

'No, it's fake snow,' Molly whispered.

'I'm going to spray snowflakes on the
window as a surprise for everyone.'

Flame blinked at her. 'What is
snow?'

Molly looked at him in surprise –
maybe it didn't snow where Flame came
from. 'It has to get very cold and then
rain freezes in pretty patterns and white
snowflakes float down from the sky. It's

so beautiful,' she explained. 'I'm really hoping for a white Christmas.'

Flame's emerald eyes widened in astonishment. 'Snow comes from the sky? I would like to see it very much.'

'I'll show you what it looks like!' Molly held the can up to the window and gently pressed the button. Nothing happened, so she shook the can hard and then tried again. Just then, someone tapped her on the shoulder.

'Molly, have you –' Shona began.

Molly lifted her finger as she turned round, but a blast of white foam shot out with a loud whooshing sound. 'Oh, heck! The button's stuck!' she gasped, jabbing at the nozzle to free it.

Shona gave a loud shriek as a powerful jet of fake snow shot all over her jumper.

★ Chapter ★
FOUR

Molly finally managed to stop the can spraying. She gaped at Shona in horror.

A thick layer of fake snow covered her from her neck to her waist. It was dripping off the ends of her long blonde hair and splatting on to the floor in soggy white blobs.

'Um, sorry . . .' Molly said lamely.

'You stupid idiot!' Shona howled. 'Look at my hair! It's ruined!'

There were muffled giggles from Narinder and some other girls, but Molly didn't laugh. She felt terrible.

Miss Garret hurried over and began mopping up the sticky mess with handfuls of paper towels. 'Calm down, Shona, this stuff washes out.' She turned to Molly. 'Whatever were you doing, messing about with that spray can?'

'I was going to make snowflakes on the windows, but the nozzle got stuck,' Molly explained.

'Oo-oh, you fibber!' Shona burst out. 'She did it on purpose, Miss! She aimed right at me and did a big long squirt! She's just jealous because I've got new

boots *and* I'm having a pony for
Christmas!'

Molly blinked at Shona in disbelief. 'I
couldn't care less about your rotten
boots and your stupid old pony!'

'That's enough, both of you!' Miss
Garret said, frowning. 'I'll speak to you
about this later, Molly. Come to the

cloakroom, Shona. We're going to have
to wash your hair and jumper. The rest
of you had better go into the hall. The
play's about to start.'

Molly hung back as Miss Garret and
Shona and most of her classmates filed
out. 'Can I help it if the spray can
decides to have a wobbler?' she said
to Flame.

'It was very bad luck,' Flame mewed
sympathetically. 'I am sorry that I could
not use my magic to help you.'

'That's OK. I know you couldn't give
yourself away,' Molly said.

Narinder ran up, grinning widely.
'That was *so* hilarious! Serves that
snooty Shona right. Stick to your story
about spraying her accidentally and
you'll be OK!'

'But it really was an accident,' Molly protested.

'Yeah, right!' Narinder said. 'I'm going to the loo. See you in the hall.'

'But . . .' Molly gave up. 'Come on, Flame,' she whispered, shrugging. 'I bet you've never seen a school play.' As she went into the corridor, Flame scampered along at her heels.

Molly almost bumped into two older girls who were waiting just outside the classroom. She recognized them as Alice and Jane, two girls from the class above hers. They both lived near Shona and often hung out with her.

Alice was tall and thin and Jane was smaller with glasses.

As Molly went to walk past, Alice

stuck out a skinny leg, so Molly almost tripped over. 'Oops. Sorry. It was an accident,' she sneered.

'Yeah! Like what you did to Shona,' Jane piped up, glaring at Molly through her glasses. 'You'd better watch your back, you little squirt!'

'Whatever!' Molly said, shrugging,

but her heart beat fast as she walked quickly away from the bigger girls.

Molly tried to enjoy the school play. The younger kids were really cute in their angel wings and tinsel halos, but Alice and Jane's threat was still on her mind.

The rest of the day seemed to drag and Molly only managed to eat a tiny bit of her school dinner, even though it was turkey with all the trimmings. The moment the school bell sounded, Molly headed for the cloakroom.

'Come on, Flame, can you quickly jump into my bag again? We don't want to bump into those two mean girls!' she urged.

She said a hurried goodbye to

Narinder at the gate. 'Sorry I'm in such
a rush. I've, er . . . got to hurry home
today,' she gabbled. 'I'll phone you!'

Narinder looked surprised. 'OK. See
you!' she said, waving.

To Molly's relief, the bus was waiting
at the bus stop. She managed to jump
on to it, just before it pulled away. She
reached home safely and was hanging
her school bag in the hall when her
mum appeared from upstairs.

'Hello, love. You look a bit glum. Is
something wrong?' Mrs Paget asked.

'I . . . um, had a bit of an accident,'
Molly began. She told her about
spraying Shona. 'And everyone thinks I
did it on purpose!'

'But of course you didn't!' Mrs Paget
said indignantly. 'You sometimes act

without thinking first, but you haven't got a mean bone in your body!' She gave Molly a hug. 'Don't worry yourself about it. It'll all be forgotten about by next term.'

'Do you think so?' Molly asked, biting her lip.

'Definitely,' Mrs Paget said firmly. She turned towards the plain white

Christmas cake on the kitchen table. Icing pens, food colouring and marzipan lay next to it. 'How would you like to decorate the cake for me? I was about to make a start on it, but I really need to nip out to the shops.'

'Cool!' Molly said, immediately cheering up. 'Just leave it to me, Mum!'

As soon as she'd waved goodbye to her mum, Molly came back into the kitchen and began making a marzipan robin. Flame sat on a kitchen chair, watching in fascination as she put the robin on the cake and then made wriggly lines with the icing pens.

Molly looked down at her work so far. 'Not bad. But it needs something else,' she said, frowning. 'I know! I'll make a snowman. I wonder if Mum's got any of that white ready-made icing stuff left.'

Climbing on to a kitchen chair, she peered into the cupboard above the table. She stood up on tiptoe and poked about behind a stack of tins. 'I can't see any –'

'Look out!' Flame mewed warningly as Molly's elbow brushed against the tins.

It was too late. Three heavy tins fell out and landed right on the cake. Thud! The cake broke apart and icing and bits of fruit cake shot all over the table.

'Oh, no!' Molly groaned in dismay.

Flame stood up on his back legs and rested his front paws on the table.

'Do not worry, Molly. I will help you,' he purred.

Molly felt a warm tingling down her spine as bright sparks ignited in Flame's silky white fur and his whiskers crackled with electricity. He lifted a tiny glittering white paw and sent a laser beam of silver sparks towards the ruined cake.

As Molly watched, the sparkling beam moved back and forth, forming the cake back into shape from the bottom up. 'Wow! It's just like watching special effects in a sci-fi movie!' she said delightedly.

The cake was half built up again, when Flame's sparkling ears twitched. 'Someone is coming!' he warned.

A second later, Molly heard the front

door slam and voices echoed in the hall. 'Hello, is anyone in? Surprise, surprise!' called Gran Paget.

'Oh, golly!' Molly gasped in panic, jumping down from the chair. 'What's she doing here? Do something, Flame!'

★ Chapter ★
FIVE

Flame's whiskers crackled with another bright burst of power.

As Molly watched, everything went into fast forward. The laser beam whizzed back and forth, re-forming the cake in treble quick time. Whump! The cake plonked itself on the plate. Whoosh! The tins zoomed into the air. One, two, three – they stacked

themselves in the cupboard. Slam! The
cupboard door closed.

Just as the last fizzing spark faded
from Flame's white fur, Gran Paget
came into the kitchen. Gramps and
Molly's dad were with her.

'Gran! Gramps!' Molly cried, hugging
them each in turn.

'Hello, love,' Gramps said, kissing her cheek. 'I bet you weren't expecting us, were you? We arranged to come a few days early to do some shopping and sightseeing. Your dad's just picked us up from the train station.'

'I wanted it to be a surprise. I don't know how I managed to keep it a secret,' Mr Paget said, grinning at his daughter.

A small flicker of unease rose in Molly's mind. 'Er. . . Dad? Does Mum know about this?' she whispered to him.

'Not yet. But she's going to be delighted. I can't wait to see the look on her face!' he replied.

Neither can I, Molly thought, remembering the state the spare room was in.

She heard the front door slam. 'I'm back,' called Mrs Paget.

'Uh-oh,' Molly breathed, running out to meet her mum and almost colliding with her. 'Guess who's here! Gran and Gramps!'

Mrs Paget almost jumped out of her skin. She dropped one of her bags and shopping began rolling everywhere. 'Molly! Do you have to dart about like that?' she scolded.

'Oops, sorry!' Molly apologized, picking up the groceries.

Her dad and grandparents came out of the kitchen to help and soon everyone was laughing. Mrs Paget hugged the grandparents. 'What a lovely surprise,' she said, looking hard at her husband.

'Time for a cup of tea and a mince pie!' Mr Paget said hurriedly.

'I'll fill the kettle,' Molly said, rushing back into the kitchen.

Her mum followed her in. As she caught sight of the Christmas cake, she stopped dead. 'Molly? Are you responsible for this?' she exclaimed.

'Um . . . yes. Sorry it didn't turn out very well . . .' Molly said over her shoulder. She was so grateful that Flame had put the cake back together in the nick of time that she had completely forgotten about the lop-sided robin and messy squiggles of icing.

'But it's wonderful!' her mum said. 'What a lovely snow scene, with a robin on a fence, and I love the snow kitten. Clever old you!'

Snow kitten? Molly spun round.

A big grin broke out on her face as she saw that the cake was even better than before the cans had fallen on it. She bent down to look under the table where Flame was sitting. 'Thanks, Flame,' she whispered.

Flame winked at her and began purring loudly. Suddenly he gave a startled yowl as a pair of arms shot under the table and grabbed him.

'How did that naughty cat get in?'
Gran scolded. 'You're going outside,
right now! Animals have no place in
kitchens!' Before Molly could react,
she opened the back door, plonked
Flame outside, and shut the door
firmly.

Molly gaped at her. 'But it's cold out
there! And Flame's only a tiny kitten!'
she protested.

'He'll be fine. He's got a nice thick
fur coat to keep him warm,' Gran said,
dusting off her hands.

Molly scowled. She marched across
and opened the back door. 'Flame's
my kitten. If he has to stay outside,
I'm staying with him!' she said
stubbornly.

'Now, Molly. Don't be hasty . . .' her mum warned gently.

'I don't care what anyone says!' Molly fumed. 'I'll stay out here all night if I have to!' She picked Flame up and cradled him against her. She could feel him trembling. 'Flame lives in the house. Tell her, Mum.'

'Calm down, Molly. I expect your gran thought Flame was just a stray who'd got in somehow. She wasn't to know you had a new kitten and I don't suppose your dad thought to tell her,' Mrs Paget said reasonably. She turned to Gran. 'Molly's right. Flame does live in the house. He's a very clean kitten.'

Gran drew herself up. She didn't look pleased. 'Have it your way then, but I'm

afraid I don't hold with spoiling pets.
They have to learn their place.'

Yes, and Flame's place is with me, Molly
thought crossly. She stormed out of the
kitchen and hurried up to her bedroom
with Flame.

She curled up on her bed and lay
there cuddling Flame and feeling
miserable. Gran hated Flame. It was
unbelievable. How could anyone not
love her gorgeous kitten as much as
she did?

'It's not fair!' she complained, stroking
Flame's fluffy white fur. 'Now you'll
have to be shut in my bedroom all the
time Gran's here.'

Flame's bright eyes sparked with
mischief. 'I do not think so! **R**emember how I came to school

with you. No one knew that I was there, did they?'

A slow, delighted grin spread across Molly's face. Of course, Flame could make himself invisible whenever he wanted to!

Molly woke early the next morning and turned over to stroke Flame who was curled up beside her. *Strange,* she thought, *something seems different.*

'Listen? Can you hear anything?' she said to him.

Flame lifted his head and yawned sleepily. 'I cannot hear anything.'

'Exactly!' Molly cried. She jumped out of bed, threw open the curtains and peered out of the window. 'Oh! It looks so beautiful,' she gasped.

The garden looked as if someone had thrown a thick white blanket all over it. Snow had made bushes and flower beds into soft blurry humps. Everything gleamed brightly under a clear silver sky.

'Hurrah!' Molly did a little dance of happiness. 'It *is* going to be a white Christmas this year! Flame! Come and look. It's been snowing overnight.'

Flame bounded across to the window sill in a single leap. He stared out at the garden with shining eyes. 'Snow is very beautiful,' he purred happily, his warm kitten breath fogging the glass.

'Come on, Flame. I'm going to ask Mum and Dad if we can go sledging in the park!' Molly decided, already

searching for a warm jumper and
old boots.

She found her dad in the sitting
room, finishing his breakfast cup of tea.
'Sledging in the park's a great idea,' he
said when Molly had finished speaking.
'I'd rather come with you, but your
mum's promised to take Gran and
Gramps for a mooch about in the
big stores.'

'Poor you!' Molly said, grinning at
the look on his face. 'Never mind, we
can go sledging another day.'

She was about to go out, when some
new knitted cushions caught her eye.
One had lime green and purple stripes
and the other had orange and blue
checks. 'Wow! Where did those come
from?' she asked.

'They were a present from your
gran. She's mad about knitting,' her dad
said wryly. 'They look . . . um . . .
interesting with our red sofa, don't
they?'

'Well, you can't miss them!' Molly
spluttered with laughter. 'I think I'll
phone Narinder and ask her if she
wants to meet Flame and me at the

park,' she decided when she could speak again. 'Have a nice time shopping, Dad.'

'I'll try to,' he said mournfully. 'See you later. Come back home by lunchtime, love.'

'OK,' Molly answered, skipping into the hall.

Ten minutes later, she was bundled up in a warm coat, scarf and gloves. 'Come on, Flame. Let's go and meet 'Rinder,' she said, opening the front door.

Flame leapt straight out and then gave a mew of surprise as he sank into the snow. He gambolled about, jumping sideways and then he stopped to sniff at the snow. 'It tastes delicious,' he purred happily, nibbling a bit.

Molly laughed as she watched him.

Sometimes it was hard to remember that this cute playful kitten was a majestic lion prince. 'It might be best if you ride on the sledge,' she decided. 'We'll get there faster and your feet will stay warm.'

'My magic will keep me warm,' Flame mewed, but he sprang on to the boat-shaped, red plastic sledge like Molly suggested and settled d own.

Molly set off, dragging her sledge and Flame behind her.

The park was only a couple of minutes away. Lots of kids were already there. Some had sledges and others sat on tin trays or plastic bags as they slid down the snowy slopes. Molly saw Narinder waving as she came

towards her. 'Hi! Isn't this brilliant!'
she cried.

'Yeah! I love snow!' Molly said.

'Hey, I didn't know you had a kitten.
Isn't he absolutely gorgeous! Where did
you get him from?' Narinder said,
bending down to stroke Flame's fuzzy
little head.

Flame purred and rubbed against Narinder's gloved hand.

'I haven't had him long,' Molly said quickly, hoping to avoid awkward questions. 'Come on. Let's go sledging!'

She and Narinder trudged up the steep snowy slope with their sledges. At the top, Molly sat down and Flame jumped into her lap.

'I'll race you!' Molly said to Narinder.

'You're on!' Narinder shouted back. 'Ready? One. Two. Three!'

'Hold on, Flame! Here we go!' Molly cried, pushing off with her hands.

Molly and Narinder flew down the slope, side by side. Flame's silky white fur blew back in the cold air.

'Whe-ee-e!' Molly yelled, grinning

across at Narinder as her sledge edged forward. 'We're winning!'

Suddenly, near the bottom of the slope, she felt the sledge skidding sideways. The front of it clipped a small bank of snow and it spun round and tipped over. Molly shot into the air and landed in the soft powdery snow with Flame still on her lap.

Narinder whizzed past, yelling triumphantly.

'Next time!' Molly shouted. Giggling, she started to get up. 'Wasn't that brilliant, Flame —'

'Well if it isn't that snotty little squirt who sprayed stuff all over me in class!' said a voice. Shona Lamb stood there with her hands on her hips. She wore a smart pink ski jacket and fluffy ear-muffs. 'Listen to her talking to her kitten. As if it's going to answer her!'

Molly's tummy gave a horrid little lurch as she saw that Shona wasn't alone. Alice and Jane, Shona's mean older friends were with her.

★ Chapter ★
SIX

'Now you're for it!' warned Shona, scooping up a big snowball.

'Yeah!' Jane said, bending down and making a snowball too.

'Three on one isn't fair!' Molly said in a wobbly voice as she got to her feet. She quickly placed Flame on the sledge out of harm's way. He stood there, tiny legs planted wide,

his fur and bushy tail bristling with
fury.

'Tough!' Alice said, grinning nastily.

Molly's mouth dried. Flame might
want to help her, but he couldn't use
his magic without giving himself away.
Narinder was at the bottom of the
long slope.

She was on her own.

A snowball hit Molly on the arm, but the powdery snow broke and it didn't really hurt. Another one landed on her back and then one hit her ear with a stinging blow. Molly hardly had time to make a snowball of her own and throw it, before she was hit again.

'Ow!' she cried as another snowball hit her neck and icy snow trickled inside her coat collar. 'That's enough now. You've paid me back,' she said, trying hard not to cry.

'Maybe she's right,' Shona said uncertainly. 'Let's go.'

'No, wait! I haven't finished with her yet!' Jane had a mean hard look on her face. She was patting her gloved hands together, making a snowball into a firm lump. Before Molly realized what she was going to do, Jane drew back her arm and aimed at Flame.

'No!' Molly screamed, throwing herself in front of him. The hard snowball smacked into her cheek with bruising force.

Molly gasped, stunned. Her cheek felt as if it was on fire and she felt sick and dizzy.

'Now you've really hurt her!' Shona said worriedly. 'She's gone all white and shaky!'

Jane and Alice exchanged glances. 'Leg it!' Jane said.

Shona came over to Molly. 'Are you all right? I'm sorry. I didn't mean it to go so far,' she said, biting her lip.

'Just leave me alone,' Molly murmured shakily.

As Shona ran after her friends, Molly's legs gave way and she sank on to the snow. Flame scampered up to her in an instant. 'Quick, Molly. Put me inside your coat,' he mewed urgently.

Molly did so. As soon as Flame was hidden from sight, Molly heard a faint crackling as sparks ignited in his fur and there was a soft glow from inside her coat as Flame's whiskers fizzed with power. The familiar warm tingling spread down her back and Molly felt a gentle prickling in her sore cheek. The pain drained away, just as if she had poured it down the sink.

'That's much better. Thanks, Flame,' she whispered.

Flame touched her chin with his tiny cold nose. 'You saved me from being badly hurt, Molly. You were very brave.'

Molly's heart swelled with a surge of affection for him. 'I'm not really. I just couldn't bear to think of anything happening to you. I love having you for my friend. I hope you can stay with me forever.'

'I will stay for as long as I can,' Flame purred gently.

'Molly! Are you all right?' Narinder's breath puffed out in the cold air as she came panting up the slope. 'I feel awful. I saw those bullies setting on you, but I couldn't get to you quickly enough to help.'

Molly grinned. 'Don't worry about it, 'Rinder, it's hard to run uphill in the

snow. Anyway, I'm OK. And I reckon
they'll leave me alone now they've had
their own back. Come on, let's go back
up. I'm definitely going to beat you to
the bottom this time!'

'Hi, we're home!' Molly sang out as she
dumped her coat and boots and went
towards the sitting room.

Her mum poked her head round the door. 'Shh. Can you be quiet, love? Gran's having forty winks in there. We've just been on a long hunt for some special knitting wool and she's worn out. Did you have a good time in the park?'

'Great, thanks. Where's Dad and Gramps?' Molly asked.

'In the garage, pottering about,' her mum replied. 'They need a bit of light relief after all those shops! Lunch won't be long, so don't go away. It's home-made tomato soup.'

'Sounds nice.' Molly went quietly into the sitting room and sat on the sofa to read a magazine. 'There's no need to become invisible, Flame. Gran's *well* asleep. Listen!' she whispered, giggling.

Soft snores rose from the corner chair, where Gran was asleep with her knitting bag in her lap. As Molly watched, the bag slowly tipped forward and a ball of blue wool fell out and rolled across the carpet.

Flame couldn't resist. He gave a tiny eager mew and pounced on it. Play-growling and lashing his tail, he chased the ball of wool round the back of Gran's chair.

Molly bit back a splutter of laughter as Flame reappeared with the ball of wool held proudly in his mouth. He tossed his head and the trailing wool tightened. Gran's knitting seemed to jump out of the bag. On the end of the trailing wool there was now a half-finished, blue and white striped sock.

'Uh-oh. Now you've really done it!'
Molly breathed. She crept forward to
rescue the knitting. But it was too late.

Gran opened her eyes, yawned and sat
up. As she spotted Flame she gave a
gasp of horror. 'My knitting! You little
menace! What have you done? Just wait
until I get my hands on you!'

Flame laid his ears back and yowled

with panic. He tried to run away, but the wool was wound tightly round his legs, and he fell over his own feet.

Red-faced, Gran got up from the chair but Molly was already bounding across the room. She got to Flame first. 'Stop wriggling,' she scolded gently, untangling him as quickly as she could. 'That's it! You'd better scoot! Gran's on the warpath!'

Flame didn't need telling twice. Flattening his ears, he zoomed out and ran upstairs. Molly picked up the mess of wool and knitting and handed it to Gran.

Gran had a face like thunder. 'That sock's ruined and I don't fancy using the wool again after that little beggar's been chewing it. Those socks were for

your dad. I'll never have them finished
for Christmas now. I told you that
kitten would be nothing but trouble!'

'Sorry, Gran,' Molly said in a subdued
voice. *Why didn't Gran just buy socks, like
normal people did, anyway?* she thought.
'Flame didn't mean to be naughty. He
was just playing.'

'Soup's ready! Molly could you go

and tell your dad and Gramps, please?'
Mrs Paget called from the hall.

'Will do, Mum. Phew!' Molly
breathed gratefully, escaping as quickly
as she could.

★ Chapter ★
SEVEN

Molly had Flame in her shoulder bag as she walked out to the car with her dad the following afternoon. It was the day before Christmas Eve and they were all going shopping at the Christmas market in the square.

'I've been meaning to say thank you to you and Flame,' her dad said.

'What for?' Molly asked, puzzled.

'For saving me from having to wear blue and white striped socks!' he said, pulling a face.

Molly laughed and gave him a friendly shove and then her face grew serious. 'Gran was furious about having her knitting spoiled. I don't think she'll ever like Flame now,' she said sadly.

'Oh, you never know. Gran's bark is worse than her bite,' her dad said.

'Really?' Molly said; then seeing her grandparents coming out of the house, she quickly got into the car with Flame.

As her dad drove them all into town, Molly counted out her pocket money. She had been saving it up for weeks and had enough to buy gifts for everyone – including Flame. It was

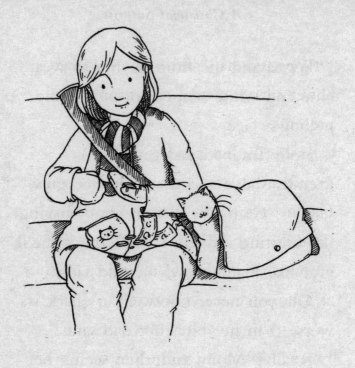

exciting to think of all the lovely things
she was going to buy.

The market was crowded and
colourful. It was full of exciting stalls,
selling things from all round the
world. Coloured light bulbs flashed on
the huge Christmas tree and tinsel
glittered under the streetlamps. People

wrapped in hats and scarves walked about carrying bags and mounds of presents.

As Molly, her parents and grandparents strolled among the stalls Flame popped his head out of her shoulder bag. His nose twitched as he enjoyed the smells of roasting chestnuts and hot spiced chocolate.

'Isn't this great?' Molly whispered to Flame, looking at some pretty silk scarves. 'I'm going to buy one of these for Mum.'

Flame didn't answer, but Molly was too busy to notice. She paused to listen to some carol singers holding lanterns, their sweet voices rising on the frosty air. At other stalls, she bought lavender bags for Gran, a key ring for Gramps and a new wallet for her dad.

'I'm doing really well with buying presents,' she said, glancing down at Flame. But his head wasn't sticking up out of her bag. 'Flame? Are you having a nap?' She reached her hand inside the bag to stroke him and her fingers brushed against a tightly curled up trembling little body. 'What's wrong?' she asked in concern.

'My uncle's spies are here. I can sense them,' Flame whined softly. 'I must hide!'

Molly's heart clenched with panic. Flame was in terrible danger. Her mind raced as she tried to decide what to do. There was no way she was letting anyone hurt Flame!

An idea jumped into her mind.
'Don't worry! We're leaving,' she
whispered to Flame.

Spotting her parents at a nearby
cheese stall, Molly dashed straight over.
'Can we go home?' she pleaded. 'I feel
awful. I think I'm going to be sick!'

Gran and Gramps appeared, holding
some parcels. 'What's wrong?' asked
Gramps.

'It's Molly. She feels ill,' Mr Paget
answered.

'It's probably all the free samples she's
tried,' Gran said. 'I expect she'll be OK
in a minute.'

'No, I won't!' Molly insisted. She
felt desperate. Rolling her eyes, she
gave a loud groan and clutched her
tummy. 'I think I'm dying! It'll be all

your fault if I collapse right here in the market.'

Even Gran looked alarmed.

'Don't be so dramatic, Molly. It's only a bit of old tummy ache,' her dad said mildly, but he looked worried. 'Perhaps we'd better take you home.'

'We've almost finished shopping, haven't we? Let's all go back,' Gramps said.

Molly could have kissed him. She flashed him a grateful smile and then remembered that she was supposed to be feeling sick.

As they all hurried towards the car park, she stroked Flame's trembling little form. 'Hang on! We'll soon be out of here,' she whispered.

Molly didn't see the dark shadowy

shapes slipping between the stalls or the narrow cruel eyes that raked the crowded market.

'He is very close,' growled a cold voice.

'Ebony will reward us well for finding the young prince,' hissed the other spy.

'I'm being allowed to stay up late tonight. We're all going to midnight mass at the cathedral. You'll love it!' Molly said happily the following afternoon.

Flame was curled up on her duvet, surrounded by bits of shiny wrapping paper, ribbons and sticky tape. He was back to his normal self, now that the danger from his uncle's spies seemed to be far behind him.

Molly was wrapping her presents in shiny foil paper. 'I hope those horrible mean cats keep on going until they jump into the sea and sink! And then you can stay with me forever,' she said to Flame.

Flame blinked up at her. 'They may come back and then I will have to leave at once. Do you understand, Molly?' he mewed seriously.

'Yes,' Molly answered in a small voice.

'But I'm not going to think about that.'

She finished wrapping her presents
and putting bows on them. 'I'll go and
put them under the tree now,' she said
to herself.

Leaving Flame dozing, she went
downstairs into the sitting room.
Gramps was reading a newspaper and
Gran was knitting. She had started a
new scarf in pink, brown and yellow
stripes.

There was the sound of voices from
the kitchen.

'Hi, Gran. Hi, Gramps,' Molly said,
bending down to put her presents with
the others. A sudden thought struck her.
Surely there was one missing. 'Oh, no,'
she gasped. 'I've forgotten to buy one
for Flame.' In all the urgency of getting

Flame away from his enemies, she'd completely forgotten to get him a present.

'What's that, love?' Gramps asked, looking up from his paper.

Molly told him. '. . . and Flame's going to be the only one without a present to open on Christmas morning,' she finished glumly.

'Oh, that's a shame,' Gran said.

Molly looked at her in surprise. It sounded like she really meant it. 'I'll just have to go to the shops and get one. Maybe Dad will take me. I'll ask him,' she said on her way to the door.

'I think it's too late, dear,' Gramps said. 'The shops all close early on Christmas Eve.'

'Oh, yes,' Molly remembered with

dismay. She stopped and turned back round. This was awful. What was she going to do? Flame would have to go without a present.

Gran looked thoughtful. 'I've got an idea,' she said, producing the scrap of blue and white sock from her knitting bag. 'I reckon I could make this into a toy mouse. I'll only take a few ticks to make some ears and a tail.'

'Do you mean it?' Molly gaped at her gran. Maybe she *did* like Flame a little bit, after all. She flew over and gave her a huge hug. 'That would be perfect! Thanks, Gran. You're the best!'

★ Chapter ★
EIGHT

Molly felt full of the magic of Christmas as she walked into the cathedral. The ancient walls flickered with the light of countless candles, and footsteps echoed on the stone floor.

Even though it was long past Molly's usual bedtime, she didn't feel a bit tired.

Flame was in her shoulder bag. And it didn't matter if everyone could see him.

Animals and their owners were all welcome for the special Christmas Eve service.

'Isn't it gorgeous in here?' she whispered to him, looking at the candlelight flickering on the stained-glass windows and the big vases of flowers and holly and ivy.

The church was packed and everyone was in a good mood. There were hot drinks, mince pies and bags of fruit and nuts to nibble. A special band with amazing instruments from all round the world played and dancers performed folk dances. And then the cathedral choir sang and everyone joined in with the carols.

Molly caught sight of Shona with her parents. She hesitated for a moment and then waved at her. Shona looked surprised and then she waved back, smiling. 'Happy Christmas!' she called.

'Happy Christmas!' Molly replied happily.

'I've got my pony. You'll have to come over and see him. He's gorgeous,' Shona said.

Molly bit back a grin. She was glad
they were friends again, but Shona
would never change.

After the service finished, Molly and
Flame, her parents and grandparents
all trudged home through the snow. A
big silver moon shed its light on to the
glittering snow crystals underfoot.

Molly held her bag close to her chest,
so that she could stroke Flame without
anyone noticing. 'This has to be the
best Christmas Eve ever,' she whispered
to him.

Just before she went up to bed, Gran
pressed a tiny package into her hand.
'For Flame. I hope he likes it,' she
said.

Molly threw her arms round her and
kissed her cheek. 'I love you, Gran.'

Gran's eyes looked moist and shiny. 'I love you too, Molly.'

Molly slipped Flame's present under the tree before she went up to her bedroom. She felt so excited that she was sure she wouldn't sleep a wink. She'd just lie there in the dark, waiting for Christmas Day.

After undressing and cleaning her teeth, Molly slipped into bed. 'Good night, Flame,' she whispered, breathing in his sweet kitten smell as she cuddled him.

Seconds later, she was asleep.

It felt like about five minutes later, when Molly opened her eyes. She was amazed to find the winter light pushing through her curtains.

'Come on, Flame. It's Christmas morning!' She leapt out of bed, threw her dressing gown on over her pyjamas and pushed her feet into her slippers.

She shot down the stairs two at a time, with Flame gambolling at her heels.

'Happy Christmas!' she said, bouncing into the sitting room.

Her mum and dad and grandparents were already dressed and sitting with hot drinks. They looked up and smiled as Molly burst in.

'Happy Christmas, love,' said her dad, pouring more coffee.

'Happy Christmas,' chorused her mum and Gran and Gramps.

'Can we open our presents now?' Molly said, going to sit cross-legged on the rug with Flame in her lap.

'We thought you'd never ask!' Gramps said. 'We've all been waiting for you to wake up.'

Molly unwrapped her presents eagerly. She had some books and music and lots of other brilliant stuff.

But best of all were the new boots she'd been hoping for. 'Cool! Thanks so much for my lovely presents, everyone!' she said, putting the boots on straight away.

'Interesting look with those pyjamas!' her dad joked.

Everyone laughed.

'Here's your present, Flame!' Molly loosened the wrapping paper.

He ripped it open with his sharp teeth and claws, a look of delight on his tiny face. The moment Flame saw Gran's knitted mouse, he gave an excited little mew. Grabbing it in his mouth he padded proudly round the room, his bushy tail held in the air.

'I'm glad someone likes my knitting!'

Gran said, giving Molly's dad one of her looks.

Mr Paget kissed Gran's cheek and then winked at Molly.

Molly choked back a laugh. 'Flame adores his mouse, Gran! Um . . . is it OK if I phone Narinder and ask if she wants to come and listen to my new CDs later on?' she asked.

'Course it is,' said her mum. 'And then can you hurry up and get dressed? Breakfast's almost ready. It's your favourite.'

'OK,' Molly said, going out into the hall.

Suddenly, Flame streaked past her and zoomed upstairs so fast that he was a tiny white blur. Molly frowned. He'd never done that before.

'Flame? What —' she broke off as a
horrible suspicion rose in her mind. She
started running after him, her phone
call forgotten for the moment.

As Molly reached the landing, there
was a bright flash from her open
bedroom door. She dashed into her

room. Flame stood there, no longer a tiny kitten, but a magnificent young white lion with a coat that glittered and glinted with a thousand sparkles. An older grey lion with a wise and gentle face stood next to him.

'Prince Flame! We must leave now!' the grey lion growled urgently.

Molly caught her breath as she understood that Flame's enemies had found him again. This time he was going to leave for good.

Flame's emerald eyes crinkled in a fond smile. 'Merry Christmas, Molly. Be well, be strong,' he rumbled in a velvety growl as a whoosh of silver sparks spun round him. And then he and the old lion disappeared.

'Goodbye, Flame. Take care. I'll never

forget you. I hope you regain your throne,' Molly said, her heart aching.

Molly knew that she'd remember this Christmas forever. Having Flame as her friend, even for only a short time, was the best present she would ever have. She stood there for a moment longer as she brushed away a tear.

And then she remembered Narinder. As Molly went downstairs to phone her, she found herself smiling.

MAGIC puppy

Snowy Wishes

My dearest puppy, Storm,

I hope this letter reaches you safe and sound. You have been so brave since you had to flee from the evil wolf Shadow.

Do not worry about me. I will hide here until you are strong enough to return and lead our pack. For now you must move on – you must hide from Shadow and his spies. If Shadow finds this letter I believe he will try to destroy it . . .

Find a good friend – someone to help finish my message to you. Because what I have to say to you is important. What I have to say is this: you must always

Please don't feel lonely. Trust in your friends and all will be well.

Your loving mother,

Canista

Prologue

Storm rolled on his back on the stony ground. The young silver-grey wolf enjoyed the scratchy feeling against his thick fur. It felt good to be back in his homeland.

Suddenly, a fierce howl rose into the air and echoed over the quiet hillside.

'Shadow!' gasped Storm. The fierce lone wolf who had attacked Storm's

Moon-claw pack was very close. He
should have known that it wasn't safe
to return.

There was a flash of bright gold light
and a silent explosion of gold sparks.
The young wolf disappeared and in its
place stood a tiny fluffy white Labrador
puppy with floppy ears and big
midnight-blue eyes.

Storm's short puppy legs trembled. He
needed to find somewhere to hide, and
quickly.

Halfway up the slope, thick bushes
clung to the rough ground. Storm
raced towards them, his little paws
kicking up spurts of dust. A dark
wolf shape was crouching near one
of the bushes. Storm's breath caught
in his throat with terror and he

skidded sideways in an attempt to escape.

'In here, my son,' the wolf called in a deep gentle growl.

'Mother!' Storm yapped with relief.

He stopped and raced back towards the bush where she was hiding. As he reached her, Storm's whole body wriggled and his silky little tail wagged delightedly.

Canista reached out a huge paw and gathered her disguised cub close against her warm body. She licked Storm's fluffy white muzzle. 'I am glad to see you again, but you cannot stay. Shadow is looking for you. He wants to lead the Moon-claw pack, but the others will not follow him while you live.'

Storm's midnight-blue eyes sparked

with anger and fear. 'He has already killed my father and litter brothers and wounded you. I will fight Shadow and make him leave our lands.'

Canista showed her strong sharp teeth in a proud smile. 'Bravely said, but Shadow is too strong for you and I am still weak from his poisoned bite and cannot help you. Go back to the other world. Hide there and return when you are wiser and your magic is stronger.'

Storm whined softly. He knew his mother was right, but he hated to leave her.

He huffed out a warm puppy breath that glittered with a thousand tiny gold sparks. The healing mist swirled round Canista's paw and then sank into her thick grey fur.

'Thank you, Storm. The pain is much better,' she rumbled softly.

Suddenly, another terrifying howl rang out and there came the sound of enormous paws thudding up the slope towards them.

'I know you are there, Storm. Let us finish this!' growled a harsh cruel voice.

'Go now! Save yourself!' Canista urged.

Storm whimpered as he felt the power gathering inside his tiny form. Bright gold sparks ignited in his fluffy white fur. A bright gold light spread around him. And grew brighter . . .

★ Chapter ★
ONE

'Robyn, love. Are you awake?'

At the sound of her mum's voice in the doorway, Robyn Parsons sat up slowly. Her bunk was moving very slightly with the motion of the ship. From somewhere deep below her she could hear the faint rumbling of the *Sea Princess*'s enormous engines.

'I wasn't asleep. I was just resting,'

Robyn murmured. 'Uh-oh,' she breathed
as her tummy gave a familiar lurch.

'Still feeling weak and wobbly?' Mrs
Parsons said gently. 'Poor old you.
That's nearly two days you've been
stuck in here.'

'I know,' Robyn said glumly, feeling
very down in the dumps.

She'd been looking forward to this
Christmas even more than usual.

Robyn didn't have any brothers or sisters and her dad worked away from home a lot. This was the first chance for ages to spend lots of time with him and they would be all together as a family.

'I think we deserve a holiday with guaranteed snow, fairy lights and lots of atmosphere! Leave it to me,' Mr Parsons had declared.

And now here they all were, all aboard the *Sea Princess* for a winter cruise round the wild and beautiful coast of Norway.

Robyn sighed. At this rate, she was going to be lucky if she caught a glimpse of any snow-capped mountains through the cabin window, let alone spend any time with her dad. It looked

like this was going to be another lonely
Christmas after all.

'How come you and Dad are OK?
I can barely even stand up without
wanting to be sick,' she grumbled.

'It's just sheer bad luck,' her mum
said sympathetically. 'We had no idea
that you'd react so badly to a sea

voyage or we'd have chosen a different way of spending Christmas.' She handed Robyn a glass. 'Have a drink of water. It might help.'

Robyn sipped the water. She felt a tiny bit better after having a drink. 'Thanks, Mum. I think I might stay sitting up. Maybe I'll look through that music magazine you got me. Where's Dad?'

'In the sun lounge, reading his paper. Are you sure you wouldn't like me to bring you something? Maybe a sandwich or some fruit?'

At the thought of food, Robyn pulled a face. 'I couldn't eat a thing.'

Mrs Parsons shook her head slowly. 'I'm really starting to wonder whether we shouldn't get off the ship at the next port and arrange to take you home.'

'No! You can't!' Robyn said at once and then wished that she hadn't spoken so loudly. Her head felt as if it was spinning. 'Dad will be so disappointed if we waste this holiday. And you've been really looking forward to it for ages.'

'So have you, love,' her mum reminded her gently. 'This was supposed to be a really special Christmas together, remember?'

Robyn nodded. 'I know, but we'll have lots more of them,' she said, trying hard to hide her disappointment for her mum's sake. 'I don't see why you and Dad can't still have a good time. I'll be fine in here by myself. I'm nearly ten years old, aren't I? And I

have to start feeling better soon. No
one stays seasick forever!'

Mrs Parsons shook her head slowly.
'I'm still not happy about leaving you
alone. I'm just going to pop back to have
a word with your dad. Let's see what he
has to say about this. I won't be long.'

Robyn's shoulders slumped as the
cabin door closed. Even though it
wasn't her fault that she felt so ill, she
knew she'd feel really guilty if their
cruise was cut short.

'It's just not fair! I'm so fed up of
being sick!' she grumbled to herself.

She took a deep breath and decided
to get up. Maybe her mum and dad
would change their minds about taking
her home if she could convince them
that she was feeling stronger.

Pushing back her quilt, Robyn slowly swung her legs over the side of her bunk. Her head swam a bit, but she stood up determinedly and reached for her jeans and fleece top. She was a bit wobbly on her feet, but she took her time getting dressed and finally managed it OK.

'I'm much better. I'm fine,' she told herself determinedly as she bent down to pull on her trainers. Suddenly, a strong dizzy feeling washed over her and she lost her balance.

'Oh,' Robyn gasped, toppling forward.

She threw out her arms, ready for a painful bruising landing, when a brilliant golden flash and a shower of sparks lit up the small cabin. Time seemed to stand still and a warm

tingling sensation ran down Robyn's
spine. She felt a sudden jolt, but there
was no hard landing.

To her complete astonishment Robyn
found herself sprawled full length on her
tummy on a sort of bouncy raft, made
of shimmering gold-coloured bubbles,
and whizzing all around her was an
ice-storm of spinning glittering sparks.

Robyn caught her breath as she felt herself slowly rising up into a sitting position and then being lowered gently on to the floor. The bubble raft and sparks dissolved with a loud crackling noise, like crisp wrappers being crumpled up.

Robyn sat there shakily on the floor and looked around nervously.

What had just happened? She felt like pinching herself to see if she had been dreaming.

'I hope you are not hurt,' woofed a strange little voice.

Robyn nearly jumped out of her skin. 'Who said that?' She twisted round, her eyes searching the small cabin.

Crouching on top of the neat chest of drawers opposite, Robyn saw a tiny fluffy white puppy, with cute floppy ears, a silky white tail and midnight-blue eyes. Thousands of tiny diamond-bright golden sparkles glittered in its thick fur.

★ Chapter ★
TWO

Robyn's eyes widened. Her mum must have brought the cute toy in to cheer her up and then forgotten to tell her about it. She must be more affected by her seasickness than she'd realized – first she'd imagined floating on a sparkly bubble raft and now she thought she'd heard this toy puppy speak to her!

Robyn stood up and went to reach

out towards the toy. 'Hello. Aren't you gorgeous? I wonder where Mum found you.'

'I came here by myself,' the puppy woofed. 'When you fell I used my magic to stop you being hurt. I am sorry if I startled you.'

Robyn gasped and pulled her hand back as if it had been burned. 'You . . . you *can* talk!' she cried.

The puppy blinked up at her with wide midnight-blue eyes. Despite its tiny size it didn't seem to be afraid of

her. 'Yes. I am Storm of the Moon-claw
pack. What is your name? And what is
this strange moving place?'

'Robyn. Robyn Parsons. And we're on
a ship called *Sea Princess*. I'm here on a
Christmas cruise with my parents,' Robyn
explained, her mind still whirling. She
found it difficult to take all this in, but
she didn't want to scare the amazing
puppy away. 'Um . . . I don't know what
you did just now, but thanks for helping
me. I could have hurt myself badly.'

'You are welcome,' Storm yapped.

Robyn slowly backed up to the edge
of her bunk and then sat down. 'Sorry,
I'm feeling a bit sick. I've been like this
since we came on board.'

Storm's little pointed face clouded
with concern. 'I will make you better.'

Robyn instantly felt another warm tingling sensation down her back as Storm reached out one little fluffy white paw and sent a fountain of tiny sparks towards her. They whirled round her, humming like tiny worker bees before disappearing. She felt the sickness washing downwards and draining out of her toes, just as if she'd been standing under the flow of a warm shower.

'Wow! That's amazing,' she cried delightedly, jumping up. 'I don't feel sick any more and I'm not dizzy or anything! Thanks again, Storm!'

'That is good.' Storm grinned, showing his sharp little teeth, and then his face took on a serious expression. 'I need to hide now, Robyn. Can you help me?'

'I'd love to, but why do you need to do that?' Robyn asked, looking down at the cute white puppy who was beginning to tremble all over.

Storm's midnight-blue eyes darkened with anger. 'An evil lone wolf attacked our Moon-claw pack – he is called Shadow. Shadow killed my father and litter brothers and wounded my mother. He wants to lead our pack, but the others are waiting for me.'

'But how can you lead a wolf pack? You're a tiny pu–' Robyn began.

'Stand back, please!' Storm interrupted.

There was a dazzling flare of golden light, which blinded Robyn for a moment. For a second or two she couldn't see anything. But when her

sight cleared the cute white puppy
had gone and in its place a
magnificent young silver-grey wolf
stood proudly, almost filling the whole
of the tiny cabin. Its thick neck-ruff
glittered all over as if it had been
dipped in gold dust.

Robyn caught her breath and would
have backed away if there had been
room. 'Storm?' she gasped, eyeing the

young wolf's sharp teeth, strong muscles and huge powerful paws.

'Yes, it is me. Do not be afraid. I will not harm you,' Storm replied in a deep velvety growl.

Robyn had hardly got used to the great majestic wolf, when there was a final flash of dazzling light. A shower of bright sparks crackled harmlessly down around her and Storm reappeared as a cute fluffy white puppy.

'Wow! You really are a wolf! That's an amazing disguise,' Robyn whispered.

Storm tucked his little white tail between his legs and Robyn saw that he was beginning to tremble again. 'Shadow will recognize me if he finds out I'm here and then he will use his magic against me. Please will you help?'

Robyn's soft heart went out to the tiny scared puppy. She bent down and stroked his soft little head. Storm was impressive as his real self, but in his cute puppy disguise he was totally adorable.

'Of course I'll help you and —' Robyn stopped as she realized something. 'Oh, I don't think animals are allowed on board. I could try to hide you in my cabin, but it's only small and you'll be really bored if you have to stay in there for the whole time.'

'I can come everywhere with you. I will use my magic so that only you can see and hear me,' Storm woofed eagerly. A couple of tiny sparks danced round his floppy white ears and then blinked out. 'It is done.'

'You've made yourself invisible? Cool!' Robyn said delightedly. She picked Storm up and gave him a cuddle. His white fur was thick and silky and smelled of cold fresh air. 'Let's go and explore *Sea Princess* together!'

'I would like that!' Storm's little white muzzle wrinkled in a smile and he licked her chin with his pink tongue.

'I can't wait to go and find Mum and Dad and tell them about you.' Robyn smiled down at him.

'No!' Storm's face was suddenly serious. 'You can never tell anyone my secret. Promise me,' he woofed gently.

Robyn felt disappointed that she couldn't share the news about her wonderful new friend with her parents – she was sure they would love him too. But if it would help to keep the tiny puppy safe, Robyn decided to keep this secret to herself.

'OK. I won't say anything. Cross my heart.'

'What's this promise you're making?'
said Mr Parsons, coming into the cabin.

'Dad!' Robyn whirled round in shock
to see her mum and dad standing there.
She'd been so busy talking to Storm
that she hadn't heard the cabin door
open. 'I was just promising . . . erm . . .
myself,' she said, thinking quickly. 'That
I was . . . um . . . going to have the

best time ever, now that I feel better. Because I've got lots of time to make up, haven't I?'

'You certainly have,' her dad said, looking surprised but delighted. 'Well, I must say that you seem to have made a miracle recovery. And there your mum was, wondering whether we ought to take you home!'

Robyn still couldn't quite believe that her mum and dad hadn't noticed Storm in her arms. But when neither of them said anything about the tiny puppy, she felt herself starting to relax.

'No one's going home. So there!' Robyn exclaimed, her eyes shining.

She spun round and pretended to straighten her duvet, giving Storm the chance to jump on to her bunk.

When Robyn turned back to her parents, her mum was beaming at her. 'I can hardly believe it. You're like a totally different girl to the one I was talking to just a few minutes ago. It's just like magic!'

If only Mum knew how right she was, Robyn thought, smiling inwardly.

'Well, you look ready to leave the cabin at last. I expect you'd like a look around to see what you've been missing. Where do you fancy going?' her dad asked.

Robyn's tummy rumbled and she realized that she was starving.

'Lunch it is, then!' said her mum.

As Robyn followed her parents to an upper deck, Storm trotted invisibly at her heel. Robyn had a warm glow

inside. After a false start, her holiday
was just beginning and she now had
a wonderful new friend to share it
with too.

★ Chapter ★
THREE

'Doesn't everywhere look great?' Robyn said to Storm. 'It makes me feel all Christmassy.'

They were walking across a part of the ship with a domed ceiling and large picture windows, swathed with evergreen garlands. Lanterns and traditional decorations made of wood and tin were strung around the walls

and Christmas trees in pots gleamed
with hundreds of fairy lights.

Robyn peered through one of the
large windows. The Norwegian sky was
filled with a strange dark-grey light and
the heavy rolling sea looked like a sheet
of ridged silver.

'It's really weird to think that it never
gets completely light during the day in
winter. I don't know if I'd like to live
here all year round,' she whispered to
Storm. 'But it looks amazing, doesn't it?
Like something out of a fairy story. You
can just imagine scaly monsters in the

sea and fierce trolls and frost giants
living in the mountains.'

'Trolls and frost giants?' Storm
flattened his ears and his silky white
tail drooped.

Robyn grinned. 'Sorry. I didn't mean
to scare you. I read up about Viking
legends and stuff when I knew we were
coming here on holiday.'

Storm still seemed unsure about being
on board a ship. He reared up on to his
back legs beside her and pressed his
little nose to the window. His big
midnight-blue eyes widened and he
gave a worried little whine.

'Are you OK?' Robyn asked, wishing
she hadn't mentioned giants and trolls
now. She hadn't realized that Storm
would take her seriously.

'I think we are lost,' Storm woofed. 'There is so much grey water and sky, but I cannot see any land.'

'That's because we're looking out on to open sea on this side,' Robyn explained. 'We can go up on deck, if you like, and then you'll be able to see land and mountains.'

Storm nodded, still not looking entirely happy as he jumped back down.

Robyn didn't expect that any of the magical wolves from the Moon-claw pack had ever been on a cruise ship; or on any other kind of ship for that matter. In his home world, Storm was a land animal. No wonder he was ill at ease.

'Come on, let's catch up with Mum

and Dad,' she said to Storm, changing the subject. 'I could eat a horse!'

Storm's face showed surprise. 'A horse? I have seen one of those. It is very large!'

'I know. I wouldn't really want to eat one. It's just something that people say when they're really hungry!'

Storm's little white muzzle twitched in a grin. Robyn was pleased to see that his anxious look had completely disappeared.

'I am very hungry too!' he yapped, falling into step with Robyn as she set off again.

A buzz of conversation and a riot of delicious smells greeted them as they entered the restaurant. Robyn could see her mum and dad beginning to help themselves from the food service area. She picked up a tray and joined them.

'Wow! Look at all this!' she whispered to Storm, her mouth watering. 'I hardly know what to choose.'

There was an enormous display of food with hot and cold dishes of all kinds, salads, sandwiches, puddings, cakes and baskets of fruit and chocolates. In the centre there was an entire miniature village made of iced gingerbread and an amazing ice sculpture of a polar bear.

Robyn heaped her plate with food for her and Storm, and then followed her mum and dad to an empty table. As soon as she sat down Storm jumped up on to her lap and curled up.

After almost two days of just drinking water, Robyn ate hungrily. She slipped bits of meat and fish under the table to Storm without her mum and dad noticing.

'Human food tastes very good,' Storm woofed, licking his chops when he'd finished. 'Thank you, Robyn.'

Robyn's mum and dad were wondering what to do next. 'We could

go swimming or watch a film or even
have a sauna,' her mum said. 'There's a
games room, shops, an Internet cafe and
loads of organized events too.'

'Could we go up on deck and look
at the view?' Robyn asked. If Storm
could see that they weren't far from
land, he might feel less nervous about
being on *Sea Princess.*

'Fine by me,' her mum said. 'I think
we should be steaming through a fjord
by now. It should be quite spectacular.'

Up on deck a cold wind was blowing
and Robyn wrapped her coat round
Storm to keep him warm. The tiny
puppy was peeping out from the front
opening and Robyn could feel him
snuggled against her chest, like a fluffy
hot water bottle.

Sea Princess was moving up a wide channel that had been created thousands of years ago by melting glaciers. The fjord stretched deep into the surrounding mountains. Painted wooden houses were clustered on the slopes and the towering, snow-capped tops were hidden by clouds.

Some people sat on deck in chairs, bundled up in warm blankets as they enjoyed the dramatic scenery. Others were lining the ship's rail, pointing out details to each other and taking photographs.

Robyn found a place to stand at the rail and looked down at the grey-green water, far below. 'I wonder how deep it is here,' she commented to Storm.

'Some of these fjords are twelve

hundred metres deep,' her dad said,
coming to stand beside her. 'That's as
deep as the mountains you can see.'

Robyn realized that she must have
spoken more loudly than she'd
intended to and her dad had thought
she was speaking to him. She would
have to be more careful about keeping
Storm's secret.

'That's scarily deep,' she said to her
dad.

Some way further on, the ship slowly
rounded a bend and Robyn saw a
waterfall gushing from a gorge in a
high cliff. Jagged icicles, like spears,
hung down from the rock and the
foaming curtain of water fell straight
down between them.

'Warm enough, love?' her dad asked

cheerfully. 'This icy air's really bringing the roses back to your cheeks.'

'I feel fine. I don't mind the cold that much,' Robyn said, giving her dad a hug. Storm gave a little warning squeak as he got a bit squashed between the two of them. 'Sorry!' Robyn whispered to him, when her dad broke away.

'Well, I've had enough of it for now,'

her mum said with a shiver. 'I think I
might have a sauna to warm me up.'

'That's a good idea. I'll come with
you. What about you, Robyn?' her dad
asked.

Robyn shook her head. 'No thanks.'
She didn't fancy all that hot steam and
she didn't want to leave Storm by
himself. 'I think I'll stay out here for a
while. I'll come and meet you at the
health suite.'

'All right, love,' her mum said. 'By the
way, the ship's docking at a fairly big
town this afternoon. I thought we
could all go ashore and do some
shopping.'

'Sounds great. Enjoy your sauna. See
you later,' Robyn called as her parents
walked away. Now that she felt well

enough to spend some time with her mum and dad, she definitely didn't mind wandering round by herself with Storm.

Her dad looked over his shoulder and winked at her. 'Watch out for trolls.'

Robyn grinned. 'I will!'

She didn't notice Storm shrinking further down inside her coat, his dewy eyes looking round nervously.

The fjord began to get narrower and more winding. The sides of the mountains were steeper here, without any houses or farms. Ice and snow clung to the jagged black rock face and the grey clouds seemed lower.

Robyn was quite enjoying the gloomy landscape. It was easy to believe that fierce trolls lay in wait for unwary travellers.

Suddenly, a bloodcurdling cry rang out behind her. Robyn almost jumped out of her skin and Storm yelped in terror. Robyn whipped round to see a number of hairy men with huge teeth, pointed ears and lumpy faces running towards her across the deck. They were dressed in rough fur cloaks and shaking their fists.

'Trolls!' gasped Robyn.

Storm growled, his whole body tensing inside Robyn's coat.

Robyn's heart beat fast. Some of the other passengers screamed and one little girl hid behind her dad.

And then Robyn saw one of the 'trolls' adjusting his mask and another one of them straightening his hairy wig. It was just some of the ship's crew who had dressed up to put on a special performance for the passengers.

She started to laugh. 'It's OK, Storm. It's only . . .' she began, in a reassuring voice, but it was too late.

Robyn felt a familiar warm prickling sensation down her spine as big gold sparks flowered in Storm's fluffy white fur and his ears crackled with magical power.

Something very strange was about to happen.

★ Chapter ★
FOUR

Robyn watched in complete amazement as Storm leapt out of her coat and sprang on to the deck, trailing a comet's tail of gold sparks.

He lifted one tiny front paw and sent a huge spray of glittering sparks whooshing into the icy air. Robyn saw them hang there for a second and then transform into greyish smoke, which sank down on to the trolls in the thickest mist she had ever seen.

'Hey! What's going on?' one of them cried from the middle of the dense mist.

'Oops, sorry,' said another one, as he tripped over his friend.

They couldn't see where they were going. Robyn could hear the disguised crew members staggering about and bashing into each other. The other passengers thought it was all part of the

act and began laughing and cheering them on.

But as the magical mist spread, they became swallowed up in it too.

'Follow me, Robyn! I will save you from the monsters,' Storm yapped. His little form glowed as brightly as a lantern as he scampered towards the door to the lower deck.

'Come back, Storm!' Robyn called to him above all the noise. 'They're not real trolls. They're people dressed up. It's just for fun!'

Storm stopped dead and then padded back towards her. In the little pool of light made by his magically glowing body, Robyn could see a shamefaced expression creep over his fluffy white face.

'I am sorry. I thought that you were in danger,' Storm yapped quietly, flattening his ears.

'It's OK. I know you were only trying to protect me, but I think you'd better make the fog disappear now,' she said gently.

Storm nodded.

He sent a big spurt of bright gold sparks whooshing across the deck. The sparkles were like a powerful jet spray at a car wash, magically blasting the fog into thin strands. Seconds later it all blew away on the icy wind.

The disguised crewmen stood there on the clear deck, looking puzzled. Their wigs were all crooked and their troll masks were dangling round their necks. But they soon recovered.

Straightening their costumes, they skipped round the deck, roaring and waving their arms.

Delighted applause broke out as more of the crew came on to the deck, holding trays of hot drinks, food and snacks.

'You must pay the price for entering our land,' one of the trolls boomed, grinning broadly. 'We order you to feast with us on troll brew and hot troll soup!'

As everyone began helping themselves, Robyn decided that this was a good time for her and Storm to make their exit.

Later that afternoon after *Sea Princess* docked at the harbour, Robyn, Storm

and her mum and dad went ashore.
They caught a bus to the south of the
city with lots of other people on the
cruise.

Robyn sat with Storm safely inside
the shoulder bag on her lap. He stuck
his head out to look at the broad
snow-covered streets and modern shops
and offices.

Robyn could see coloured lights
gleaming from house windows and
there were lots of green wreaths hung

on doors. Here and there, they passed
traditional wooden buildings, painted in
shades of red, orange or mustard.

'Everything looks so Christmassy here.
I love it,' she whispered. 'I hope I can
get some presents for Mum and Dad.'

Storm twisted round and looked up
at her. 'What is Christmas?'

'Oh, of course. I don't suppose you
have it in your world, do you?' Robyn
realized. 'Christmas is a special time
when we celebrate the baby Jesus being
born. We sing carols and families all get
together and exchange presents and eat
lots of yummy food. Dad usually stuffs
himself with turkey, mince pies and
cake and then moans about his trousers
being tight! At least, that's what we
usually do at home. It's going to seem

a bit different this year. We celebrate Christmas on Christmas Eve aboard *Sea Princess.*'

Storm looked a bit puzzled but his midnight-blue eyes were twinkling with excitement. 'It sounds very odd, but I think I will enjoy Christmas, especially the food!'

The bus stopped near an enormous cathedral with a towering spire and lots of amazing stone carving. Coloured light streamed out on to the snow from its stained-glass windows.

Robyn's mum produced a tourist brochure she'd picked up on the way to the bus. 'I think I'd like to look around inside that cathedral. It says here that it's getting on for a thousand years old. Imagine that!' she said enthusiastically.

'Wow!' Robyn said. She couldn't imagine anything being that old. But she didn't really fancy walking round some musty-smelling old cathedral for hours, however impressive it was. 'Do we all have to go?' she asked, without enthusiasm.

Mr Parsons smiled. 'I don't think so. I'm not as interested in old buildings as your mum. You and I'll go shopping and meet her later.'

'Oh good,' Robyn said, relieved.

'Fine,' Mrs Parsons said. 'I'm quite happy to mooch about by myself.' She turned to her husband. 'I'll see you back here in a couple of hours?'

Mr Parsons nodded. 'Sounds good.'

Robyn waved to her mum as she set off towards the cathedral and then she and her dad set off in search of interesting shops. Storm leaned up and hooked his front paws over her shoulder bag, so that he could look at the surroundings.

They had been walking for a couple of minutes when Storm reached out and tapped Robyn's arm with one front paw. She looked down to see that he'd pricked up his little ears.

'I can hear music,' he yapped.

'I can too,' Robyn whispered. 'Can you hear that, Dad?' she said in a louder voice. 'It's coming from over there.'

Mr Parsons listened. 'Oh yes. It's quite faint, but it sounds like folk music. Let's go and have a look.'

As they walked to the end of the street, the music got louder. They reached a cobbled square, surrounded by stalls, heaped with crystallized fruit, gingerbread and spiced biscuits. Cheery lanterns were strung between the buildings encircling the small square, and green garlands and decorations were looped between the stalls.

Storm yipped excitedly as he saw the bandstand, with musicians playing violins. Women in colourful felt skirts and men in waistcoats and buckled shoes were dancing. A festive smell of spiced wine and roasted nuts filled the frosty air.

'Oh, it's a Christmas festival!' Robyn exclaimed delightedly.

★ Chapter ★
FIVE

Robyn sipped a cup of hot spiced apple juice as she watched some children building snowmen. It was a competition and a number of half-built snow trolls and elves stood in one corner of the square. There was even a Father Christmas snowman with his snow reindeer.

In the strange half-light, the glowing

lanterns cast a cheerful glow over everything. Storm jumped out of Robyn's bag in another little flurry of sparks.

At first, Robyn was worried that his little paws would get cold on the frozen ground. But Storm's white ears sizzled with tiny sparks and she noticed that he was now wearing four tiny furry boots.

He looked so cute wearing them that Robyn burst out laughing, which

she quickly turned into a cough. She
didn't want to hurt her puppy friend's
feelings.

As she and her dad wandered around
the market stalls, they bought cheese,
chocolate and spice cakes for presents
to take home for Gran and Gramps.
Robyn didn't see anything she wanted
to buy for her mum and dad.

She spotted a shop a few metres away
on the other side of the square. 'I'm just
going to pop into that shop over there.
I won't be long,' she told her dad.

Mr Parsons nodded. 'All right. I'll still
be here.'

Storm scampered after Robyn as she
headed across the square. Inside the
shop it felt really warm after the cold
outside. Robyn took off her hat and

gloves and stuffed them in her coat pocket.

There were lots of people looking at the gifts and cuddly toys. Robyn noticed a rack of knitwear. Maybe her mum would like a traditional hand-knitted cardigan.

As she went to have a closer look, Robyn heard raised voices. A sales assistant was speaking sharply to a tall slim girl with black hair, who looked about twelve years old.

'I am not a thief!' the girl said in a low angry voice. She was wearing a red felt skirt, decorated with bands of embroidery and sturdy leather boots.

'We'll see about that!' the sales assistant shouted, beckoning to a man from another counter.

As Robyn stood at the far end of the long clothes rack, the man hurried over. 'What's the problem?' he asked the assistant.

'This young lady has taken an expensive *lusekofte*. See, there is the empty hanger,' the woman said crossly, pointing to the rack of knitted cardigans. 'I demand that she opens her bag so that I can search it!'

'Did you see her take it?' the man asked.

The woman put her hands on her hips. 'No. But she must have. One's missing and it was there a minute ago!'

'I told you. I have not taken it. I would never do that,' the girl said calmly, clutching her bag with two hands.

Her face was pale, expect for her cheeks, which were flushed a deep red. Robyn could see that the girl looked close to tears and admired the way she was sticking up for herself against the bossy assistant.

'That woman's determined to search the girl's bag. I hope she hasn't pinched anything,' Robyn whispered to Storm.

Suddenly, Storm's head came up and he gave a triumphant woof.

Diving beneath the rack of cardigans, the tiny puppy jumped up and ferreted about. He grabbed something and a loose cardigan came free. Storm dropped it on to the floor before padding back to Robyn.

'Oh, well done, Storm!' Robyn praised him, pleased that it looked like the young girl hadn't taken anything. 'The cardigan must have slipped off its hanger. It was lucky you spotted a bit of its dangling sleeve, Storm.' The sales assistant obviously hadn't looked carefully enough.

On impulse, Robyn picked up the empty hanger and stepped forward. 'Excuse me,' she said politely, holding it up. 'Are you looking for the cardigan that was on this?'

The two assistants and the dark-haired girl turned to look at her.

'I know where it is,' the woman snapped. 'It's inside this young person's bag!'

'Are you sure?' Robyn asked. 'Because there's one on the floor. Look.'

The assistant frowned and went to investigate. A deep flush crept up her face as she came back holding the cardigan. 'I . . . er . . . seem to have made a mistake. We'll say no more about it,' she said shortly. Snatching the empty hanger from Robyn, she marched briskly away.

The male assistant threw the girl an apologetic look and then hurried back to his counter.

Robyn's eyes widened. 'What a rotten cheek! That woman didn't even say sorry!'

'It does not matter,' the girl replied,

shrugging. 'I knew I had done nothing, but thank you for speaking up for me. I am Kristiana Magga. Everyone calls me Krista. What is your name?'

'Robyn. Robyn Parsons. I'm here on holiday with my mum and dad,' Robyn said, surprised that the girl was so calm after the unpleasant scene. She saw that Krista had high cheekbones and unusual dark eyes, which were slightly tilted at the corners.

'I am very glad to meet you,' Krista said with a wide smile.

'Me too,' Robyn said. 'Do you live here?'

Krista shook her head. 'I am visiting friends. My Uncle Nikolai and Aunt Jorun are with me. Oh, here they are now.'

A man and woman came towards them. Robyn saw that they had high cheekbones and dark hair, like Krista. Krista's aunt also wore a blue felt skirt and strong leather boots. There was a fringed gold shawl round her shoulders, pinned with a circular brooch.

'This is my new friend Robyn,' Krista said.

Robyn glowed at Krista's description of her as a friend. Since they'd only just met, it was a lovely thing to do.

Krista then told her aunt and uncle about the sales assistant who had accused her of stealing. '. . . and Robyn proved that I didn't steal it after she found the *lusekofte* on the floor,' she finished.

It wasn't me, actually, it was Storm,

Robyn thought, wishing that she could tell them all how brilliant her magic friend was. She smiled proudly at the little puppy who was sitting nearby watching, visible only to her.

'Thank you, Robyn,' Krista's aunt said. 'It's very nice to meet you. I wish we had more time to talk, but now we must go.'

'Yes. We have many things to buy before we return to our home in the north,' said her uncle.

'Goodbye, Robyn,' Krista said with a warm smile. 'Enjoy your holiday.'

'Thanks, I will. Bye, Krista,' Robyn said.

She and Storm watched as the girl and her aunt and uncle left the shop. As they walked past the glass shop front, Krista paused to wave.

Robyn waved back, feeling a little sad that she had to leave so soon. 'Krista seemed really nice, didn't she?' she said to Storm. 'What a shame that we'll never see her again.'

'I liked her too,' Storm woofed.

'Come on, Storm. Let's go and find

Dad.' She'd gone right off the idea of buying any presents from this shop.

★ Chapter ★
SIX

The next day passed quickly. *Sea Princess* sailed along through ever more majestic fjords and Robyn and Storm stood on deck to watch the spectacular scenery passing by. When the ship docked at another coastal town they went ashore with her parents to explore.

Before boarding again, she found time to dash into a shop and buy her mum

some traditional hand-knitted gloves.
She also bought her dad a wallet and
got felt slippers for her gran and
gramps. 'Great. That's my present-buying
finished.' *Except for Storm*, she thought,
wondering how she was going to buy
him a present without him seeing.

Later on Robyn, Storm and her mum
and dad sat in a cafe near the harbour.

Robyn stirred the floating blob of
fresh cream into her mug of hot
chocolate and then took a big sip.
'Mmm. Gorgeous,' she murmured,
licking her lips.

Her dad grinned around a mouthful
of cream cake. 'I'm not sure the
chocolate moustache's a good look on
you!'

'Ha ha! Very funny.' Robyn pulled a

face at him and wiped her mouth.

She scooped up a big fingerful of cream and slipped it inside her shoulder bag for Storm to lick. His warm little tongue flicked over her fingers and she hid a fond smile. She loved having Storm as her friend and sharing this wonderful holiday with him.

Robyn gazed out of the window as she nibbled a spice biscuit and found herself thinking about Krista.

Robyn had told her mum and dad

about the cardigan incident in the shop and described Krista and Jorun's lovely clothes. 'Your young friend is probably from a Sami background,' her mum guessed. 'I read in our travel guide that the Sami people used to be known as Lapps and once moved around with their herds of reindeer. A lot of them live a more settled life now.'

Robyn remembered that Krista's Aunt Jorun had said they were returning to their home in the north. She thought it must be amazing to live in a land of ice and snow, where it got so cold that even the sea froze.

Sea Princess docked at a small port the next morning and Robyn, Storm and her parents made their way to a smaller boat, which was waiting to take them to see a large glacier.

Passengers piled into the boat and lined the rails. Robyn looked down into the dark freezing water, which was so much closer to them on this small boat, and shivered. It looked very cold and very scary – she held on to the boat rail as it set off. On the way to the ice cap, the vast frozen expanse that stretched its arms down into a number of deep valleys, they sailed between islets and skerries.

Robyn was waiting excitedly for her first ever glimpse of a glacier.

'We should see it in a minute,' she whispered to Storm, who was in her shoulder bag.

Storm nodded.

Robyn was unprepared for the amazing sight that met her eyes. The frozen river, cutting through the huge snow-capped mountains, ended in a breathtaking wall of towering ice, which was reflected in the sea.

'Oh my gosh!' Robyn's jaw dropped. 'That's awesome!'

Sounds of cracking, like pistol shots,

rang out in the still air and some of the passengers looked worried. Storm whimpered and Robyn glanced down to where he sat with his front paws looped over the bag. He was twitching his ears nervously.

'That noise is just the sound of boulders getting crunched under the ice,' the guide explained to the worried passengers.

'Did you hear what that man said? It's nothing to be scared about,' Robyn whispered reassuringly to Storm. But when he continued to stare at the glacier intently, she frowned. 'Storm? Did you hear me?'

There was an extra loud *bang!* and an ominous grinding sound — Storm's entire fluffy white body tensed and his hackles rose along his back. 'There is great danger!' he barked urgently, leaping down on to the deck.

Robyn felt a familiar warm prickling flow down her spine as big golden sparks bloomed in Storm's fluffy white fur and his ears sparked with electricity. Suddenly, the little boat shot forward in a dazzling burst of speed.

Robyn grabbed hold of the rail again and clung on for dear life.

Storm whimpered as his claws skittered across the deck and he slid towards the rail, about to fall overboard into the freezing bottomless sea.

Robyn acted without thinking. Still hanging on with one hand, she swooped down and reached out. For

one heart-stopping moment, she
thought she had lost him. But then her
fingers closed on the scruff of Storm's
neck. Yes! Robyn hauled the terrified
puppy to safety and tucked his
trembling little form safely back inside
her bag.

'Thank you for saving me, Robyn!'

Storm barked, looking up at her gratefully with his big blue eyes.

'I'm just glad you're OK,' she replied, trying to stay on her feet and steady her shoulder bag at the same time.

The other passengers were bracing themselves as best they could as the small boat suddenly zoomed back out to sea in a shower of golden sparkles before stopping abruptly near one of the small islets.

'Storm! What's going on?' Robyn asked in a shaky voice.

Suddenly, there was a thunderous cracking sound and massive slabs of ice parted from the glacier and dropped into the sea with a resounding *splash!* To everyone's horror, a huge tidal wave began rushing towards the boat.

Robyn felt the colour drain from her face as the wall of water bore down on them with the speed of an express train.

Storm calmly lifted both front paws and sent another fountain of sparks whooshing across the sea at the tidal wave, which immediately sank without a trace. The small boat rocked gently as normal-sized waves brushed harmlessly against its sides.

No one else could have seen Storm's magic and the stunned passengers all began speaking at once.

Robyn looked down fondly at her little friend. 'You were amazing, Storm! We could all have been really badly hurt and you nearly were. Thank you.'

Storm gave a little shake as every last

spark faded from his thick fur. 'I am
glad I was able to help.'

'Are you all right, love?' asked
Robyn's dad, putting his arm round her
shoulders. 'I'm a bit shaken up myself!'

'I'm fine now,' Robyn said.

Beside them, Robyn's mum
shuddered. 'I dread to think what would
have happened if we'd been right under

the glacier when that sheet of ice fell off! Thank goodness the captain had the presence of mind to put on a burst of speed.'

'Whoever was responsible for saving us was very brave, wasn't he?' Robyn said meaningfully, reaching one hand into her bag to stroke Storm's warm fur.

She felt so proud of her friend. It was just a shame that no one else would ever know how wonderful he was.

★ Chapter ★
SEVEN

Robyn stood on deck, bathed in the night's moonlight, with Storm cuddled in her arms inside her coat. She was still a little nervous after saving Storm the other day and was determined to keep her little friend safe.

It had grown colder as *Sea Princess* steamed further north and this was the coldest weather Robyn had ever

experienced. The icy air prickled inside
her nose as she breathed in. It was a
strange sensation.

Storm's ears were pricked up and his
breath fogged in the air as he gazed up
at the millions of silver stars that
seemed so close you could reach out
and touch them.

'Brrr!' Robyn said, trying to hide a

shiver. She was thinking of going inside to get warm, but the tiny puppy was obviously having such a good time that she didn't want to spoil his enjoyment.

'You are cold, Robyn,' Storm noticed. 'I will make you warm.'

A familiar warm tickling sensation ran down Robyn's backbone as tiny gold sparks bloomed deep within his fluffy white coat. Instantly, she felt a thick layer of fur lining her jeans, her jacket and even her hat and gloves, and she was as warm as toast.

'Thanks, Storm, that's much better. Oh, look!' Robyn breathed in wonder as a shifting curtain of glowing greenish lights appeared and began rippling across the clear winter sky. 'Those must be the Northern Lights. Aren't they amazing?'

'They are like the lights of my homeland. We often see them in the sky,' Storm woofed softly, sounding a little sad.

Robyn wondered what Storm's home world was like. Perhaps it was a land of ice and snow too. It must be a strange and wild place, where the great magical wolves that lived there fought over their lands. She felt a pang as she thought that Storm might be homesick and thinking of his wounded mother and the scattered Moon-claw pack.

Bowing her head, Robyn kissed the top of Storm's silky little head and held him close.

'Robyn? Is it really you?' called a voice.

Robyn almost jumped out of her skin. She spun round to see the slim dark-haired girl from the knitwear shop standing there with a broad smile on her face.

'Krista!' she said delightedly. 'What are you doing here?'

Krista smiled. She wore a red parka with a fur-trimmed hood. 'I am on my way back home, with my uncle and aunt. I did not realize that you were on a cruise round the coast. We use the coastal steamers, like *Sea Princess,* as local ferries to get around.'

Robyn remembered seeing that *Sea Princess* had a ferry and car deck. 'Where do you live? Is it very far

away?' she asked, hoping that there might be time for her and Storm to get to know Krista better.

Krista told her. 'We will reach the port in two days, on Christmas Eve. My village is a short distance inland. I live there with my mother and father, my brothers and sisters and aunts and uncles and cousins and all the rest of my family. I will be very glad to see them again.'

'You live with *all* of your family?'
Robyn asked curiously. She did get a
bit lonely with her dad away a lot of
the time, but Robyn wasn't sure she'd
want to live with a whole lot of other
people. 'Do you travel about a lot after
your reindeer herds? Sorry. I didn't
mean to sound nosy. I'm just interested,'
she said, blushing as she realized that
she seemed to be asking lots of
questions.

Krista laughed. 'That is all right. At
this time of the year, we live in houses,
but others, like my grandmother and
grandfather prefer to live in a *lavvo* –
that's a traditional tent,' she explained.
'Lots of other Sami families live in the
village too. We make things to sell,
until the season for calves to be born,

and then everyone helps out with the hard work.'

'Cool,' Robyn said, fascinated. Krista's life was completely different to her own. It sounded so busy and exciting.

Krista smiled at her enthusiasm and her slanted dark eyes twinkled. 'Would you and your parents like to visit my village and meet my family?'

'Would I? I'd love it!' Robyn said at once. 'But I'll have to ask my mum and dad if it's OK. They're in the main lounge. Why don't you come with me, then you can meet them?'

Krista nodded. 'I would like that. I will go and fetch Uncle Nikolai and Aunt Jorun. They would like to meet your parents too.'

As Robyn went below decks with

Krista, she whispered to Storm. 'Isn't it great that we've bumped into Krista again?'

Storm's little face lit up and he woofed in agreement.

Robyn woke the following morning, feeling full of excitement. Storm was curled in the crook of her arm. As she stirred, he opened one eye and then tucked his nose back between his paws.

'Come on, sleepy-head!' Robyn teased, gently tickling his furry little

sides. 'We're meeting Krista for breakfast.'

Storm stuck out all four fluffy white legs and had a big stretch before jumping to the floor.

Robyn threw back the quilt and got dressed quickly. Her parents were showered and ready and they all went to the restaurant together. Robyn spotted Krista at a table the moment she and Storm walked in. She waved to her as she helped herself from the usual display of delicious food.

'Hi,' Robyn said as she went and sat next to Krista.

'Hello, Robyn. Did you sleep well?'

'Yes, thanks. Oops,' Robyn said, as she felt Storm scrabbling up on to her lap. She pretended to drop her fork and just managed to stop him from slipping off again.

The adults joined them with their plates of food. Mr Parsons and Uncle Nikolai began chatting about football. Robyn's mum and Aunt Jorun talked about knitting, having discovered that they shared a passion for handicrafts the previous night.

'They all seem to be getting along very well, don't they?' Robyn commented to Krista.

'Yes, they do,' Krista said. 'I am very pleased that your parents have accepted my invitation to visit our village.'

'Me too. I can't wait,' Robyn said eagerly.

'I'm glad you said that,' Krista replied, her eyes glinting mysteriously. 'I have told my cousin Morten that you are coming to visit. He is arranging a surprise for you.'

Robyn smiled, wondering what it could be.

★ Chapter ★
EIGHT

Later that day, Robyn and Storm
were walking past some fishing boats
frozen into the ice on a village wharf,
on their way to meet up with her
mum and dad who were in the
supermarket opposite. Robyn couldn't
stop thinking about what Krista's
surprise might be. She smiled down at
Storm happily – this was turning out

to be one of her best Christmases ever.

Suddenly, Robyn heard some furious snapping and growling. It was coming from a car parked outside a supermarket. In the back were two large dogs, who were scrabbling at the window.

Storm whimpered in terror and cowered against Robyn's legs. She could feel him trembling from head to foot through her warm boots.

'Shadow knows where I am. He has sent those dogs to attack me,' Storm whined.

Robyn tensed as she saw the street lights gleaming on the dogs' pale eyes and extra large teeth. How was she going to save her little friend? She was just about to pick Storm up and run away as fast as her legs would carry her when a man came out of the supermarket and got into the car. The fierce growling and barking eventually faded as the car pulled away.

'Those horrible dogs have gone now. You're safe with me,' Robyn said. She picked Storm up and hurried into a narrow side street.

The tiny puppy pressed himself against her and looked up at her with fearful eyes. 'For now, perhaps, but Shadow will use his magic on other dogs we meet. If any of them find me, I may have to leave quickly, without saying goodbye.'

Robyn couldn't bear to think of losing Storm so suddenly. 'Maybe if we hide you really well, Shadow will give up looking for you and then you can stay with me forever. I'll take you home with me when the cruise ends. You'll love it there.'

Storm reached up and touched her face with one fluffy white front paw.

'That is not possible. One day, I must return to my homeland to lead the Moon-claw pack. Do you understand that, Robyn?' he barked, his little face serious.

Robyn swallowed hard, but she forced herself to nod as she went back towards the supermarket. She didn't want to think about anything, except enjoying every single moment of her Christmas holiday with Storm.

Christmas Eve finally arrived and Robyn and Storm stood beside Krista as *Sea Princess* steamed into the harbour with her horn blaring. The greyish winter light hung over the small town, which banked steeply up the hillside behind the harbour.

The ship was only staying for a few hours as the Christmas festivities would soon begin on board.

'Will it take long to get to where you
live?' Mrs Parsons asked Krista.

'Not long at all.' Krista looked at
Robyn and her lips curved in another
of her mysterious smiles.

Robyn was puzzled. What could
Krista be planning?

Ten minutes later, when she and
Storm were getting off the ship, Robyn
gave a cry of delight. A beautiful
wooden sleigh, pulled by two reindeer
in brightly coloured harnesses with
woollen tassels stood waiting.

'Wow! This is fantastic,' Robyn
enthused.

'What a wonderful surprise,' her dad
said.

Krista smiled. 'I thought you would
like it. This is Morten, my cousin,' she

said, introducing the tall young sleigh driver.

'Pleased to meet you,' Robyn said, smiling.

Robyn's mum and dad greeted him and then Morten helped them climb aboard the sleigh, before helping to load the supplies.

Robyn settled Storm on her lap and they nestled beneath the warmth of the thick furs. Krista sat next to her. Once everyone was settled, Morten twitched the reins and the reindeer sped off across the snow in a jingle of sleigh bells.

'This reminds me of that "Winter Wonderland" song!' Robyn's dad said. 'In the lane, snow is glistening. Can't you hear, logs are blistering . . .'

he began, singing all the wrong
words.

Robyn saw her mum give him one
of her looks and dig him in the ribs.

Robyn stifled a giggle as her dad fell
silent. Krista glanced at her mum and
they both fell about laughing.

Storm sat upright on Robyn's lap,
looking around at the thick blanket of
white snow. More flakes began to fall,
dancing in the glow of the sleigh
lanterns.

Soon lights were visible in the gloom
ahead. Robyn saw buildings with turf

poking up through the snow on their roofs. Tall cone-shaped tents were dotted about. She could smell woodsmoke on the frosty air.

As Morten brought the sleigh to a halt, people hurried out to welcome back Krista and her aunt and uncle. Robyn smiled and shook hands as she was introduced to Krista's parents, her brothers and sisters, and countless aunts and uncles and cousins. She knew she'd never remember all of their names.

'My grandparents would like to welcome you to their *lavvo*,' Krista explained. Robyn, Storm and the adults were shown inside one of the tents.

Colourful wall hangings and a crackling log fire inside the *lavvo* made it very warm and cosy. Delicious smells came from a metal cooking pot hanging over the flames. Robyn sat down close to the fire and Storm came and curled up beside her.

Krista's grandparents made them very welcome with food and hot drinks. Afterwards, a woman entertained them with traditional chanting and storytelling, while playing on a skin drum covered with drawings.

'We call this *joik*,' Krista told Robyn. 'Storytelling is an old tradition of my people.'

Storm sat up and pricked his ears, enjoying the entertainment. 'I like this place,' he woofed.

Robyn reached down to pat him, to show that she did too. But she didn't dare risk whispering to him with all the people around.

Krista showed Robyn round her house too. It was similar to the houses back home, with a modern TV and a computer, but there was a large wooden hut and a wooden pen for reindeer attached to the side of it. Krista's mum made fabulous jewellery with silver wire.

Time passed all too quickly and soon they had to return to *Sea Princess*.

There were many goodbyes and hugs all round. Morten drove the reindeer sleigh back to the harbour and Krista insisted on coming along with Robyn to keep her company.

As the sleigh drew to a halt at the harbour beside the huge bulk of *Sea*

Princess, Krista slipped something into
Robyn's hand.

'I made this. It is for you,' she said.

Robyn looked down to see that it
was a tiny reindeer horn carving of an
arctic wolf. The tiny wolf looked just
like Storm as his real self. It even had
chips of some glittery dark-blue
material for eyes.

'Oh, it's beautiful. Thank you,' she said
warmly, giving Krista a hug.

'I am glad that you like it,' Krista said, her tilted dark eyes moist.

'I love it to bits,' Robyn said with a catch in her voice. 'Goodbye, Krista. And thanks for letting me meet your family. I had the best time ever. I'll send you an email when I get back home.'

Krista's face brightened. 'Oh yes, please do. And maybe we can talk online. It will be wonderful to keep in touch with each other.'

'Definitely!' Robyn promised. She wished this Christmas could last forever.

★ Chapter ★
NINE

Robyn stood on board *Sea Princess*
with Storm in her arms. They were
looking down at the harbour, where
Morten was turning the sleigh around.
The reindeer and Krista, huddled in
the sleigh among the furs, looked
tiny now.

Krista waved one small mitten as the
reindeer plunged forward and the sleigh

moved smoothly away on wooden
runners.

'Goodbye. Safe journey!' she called.

'Goodbye!' Robyn cried, waving.

She and Storm waited until they
could no longer hear the sound of
sleigh bells, before going inside the ship.

Robyn's mum walked beside her.
'Well, that was wonderful, wasn't it?

Krista's family were so hospitable. You must get me their address. I'd love to send them something from England when we get back.'

Robyn thought that was a great idea.

'Well, shall we go and see if anything's happening in the lounge yet? I fancy singing a few carols,' her dad said.

'Sounds great. I'll just be a minute. I want to get something from the cabin,' Robyn replied.

She was going to fetch the gloves and wallet, which were hidden at the end of her bunk. She wanted to wrap them and then sneak them under the enormous Christmas tree, so her mum and dad would be able to open them later.

Storm padded beside Robyn at her

heel as she went below decks. They had just stepped into the corridor leading to their cabin when Storm gave a yelp of terror and shot forward.

'What's wrong?' Robyn said, frowning.

Storm stood beside the cabin door, pawing frantically at it. She could see that he was trembling from head to foot.

Suddenly, Robyn heard fierce growling. Whipping round, she saw the shadows of two large dogs coming down the stairwell on the wall behind her.

Robyn's heart missed a beat. Shadow must have found Storm when they were on land and sent his dogs on to the ship after him! He was in terrible danger.

Robyn didn't think twice. She hurtled down the corridor and unlocked the cabin door with shaking fingers. She and Storm dashed inside, just as a fierce snapping and growling sounded right behind them.

'Oh!' Robyn shielded her eyes with her hand as a dazzling flash of bright light lit up the entire cabin.

Storm stood before her, a tiny fluffy white puppy no longer, but a majestic young silver-grey wolf. Hundreds of tiny diamond-bright lights glowed from his thick neck-ruff. Beside him stood a larger wolf with a gentle expression and large golden eyes.

And then Robyn knew that Storm was leaving for real.

She went forward and threw her arms

round the wolf's neck. 'I'll never forget
you, Storm,' she said.

Storm allowed her to hug him for a
moment and then gently pulled away.
'You have been a good friend, Robyn.
Be of strong heart,' he rumbled in a
deep velvety growl.

Robyn nodded, unable to speak as
she felt a tear run down her cheek. She
remembered that she hadn't been able

to get Storm a Christmas present. It seemed wrong not to give him something.

She had a sudden thought. 'Please, wait!' Reaching into her pocket, she took out Krista's gift. She held it out to Storm. 'This is for you. To remind you that, one day, you'll be a great leader of the Moon-claw pack,' she murmured.

Storm reached out and closed his huge paw over the tiny carved wolf. 'Thank you, Robyn. You are very kind.'

There was a final burst of intense gold light and a great shower of gold sparks exploded silently into the air and drifted harmlessly down around her. Storm and his mother faded and were gone.

The fierce growling outside the cabin stopped and silence fell.

Robyn felt a deep ache. She would never forget Storm, but she would always have her memories of the incredible Christmas holiday she had shared with the magic puppy.

The cabin door opened and her dad stood there. 'Oh, there you are, love. Are you coming up to the lounge? There's a carol service on and afterwards Father Christmas is going to give out presents.'

Robyn quickly dashed away a tear and smiled. 'Just coming!'

A Whole New World of Christmas Puppy Fun & Games!

Snowy Christmas Crossword

Magic puppy Storm loves finding out about Christmas
in this world! How much do you know?

Across

2 Something that you get
given at Christmas.

5 It falls out of the sky at
winter and is fluffy, cold
and white.

7 The name of a very special
magic puppy!

Down

1 A very festive time of year.

3 You decorate a Christmas
tree with this sparkly stuff.

4 He comes down the
chimney at Christmas time.

6 What kind of creature is
Storm in his own world?

Dot-to-dot

Join the dots to find a little magic friend.

13 12
16 15 14 11
17
10
18 19
20 1
3 2 9
21
8
22
7
23 4 57
6 56
5
24
55
25 54

53
26 34 47
52 48 46
35 49
27 33 50 45
32 51
28 37 36 44
31 41
29 42 43
30 38 40
39

Your Very Own Christmas Tree

You will need: ★ Green card ★ Scissors (ask an adult to help you with this tricky bit) ★ Crayons, glitter or star stickers to decorate

★ Put two pieces of rectangle-shaped card together and fold them in half long-ways.

★ Draw half a Christmas tree opposite the fold.

★ Cut along the Christmas tree line so that you get two identical trees.

★ Cut a slit down the middle of the top half of one tree and up the bottom half of the other.

★ Slip the two trees together along the splits.

★ Decorate with crayons, glitter or stars to make your Christmas tree sparkle!

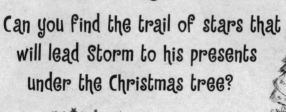

Puppy Trails

Can you find the trail of stars that
will lead Storm to his presents
under the Christmas tree?

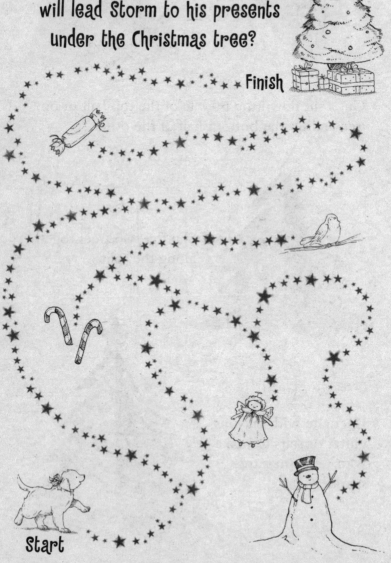

Finish

Start

Colour by Numbers

Use the key to colour in this festive Christmas scene.

Colour key:

1 green   4 blue   6 brown
2 red   5 purple   7 white
3 yellow

Spot the Difference

Can you spot the eight differences between these pictures of Storm and Robyn's magical sleigh ride?

How Many Bones?

Brrr! The chilly weather has given Storm a big appetite. How many of his delicious bones can you spot in this picture?

Draw the Missing Half

Can you finish the picture of this Christmas tree? Add as many decorations as you like then colour it in.

Christmas Crackers!

Q: Where do snowmen go to dance?

A: A snow ball!

Q: Why is it always so cold at Christmas?

A: Because it's in **December!**

Q: What is Father Christmas's puppy called?

A: Santa Paws!

Q: What do Father Christmas's elves do after school?

A: Their gnome work!

Q: What happens when you eat Christmas decorations?

A: You get tinsel-itus!

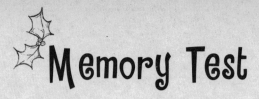

Memory Test

Look carefully at the picture, then cover
it up with a piece of paper.
How much can you remember?

1. There are three fairy dolls hanging on the wall.

True ☐   False ☐

2. There are two Christmas trees in the picture.

True ☐   False ☐

3. There is one little red robin outside the window.

True ☐   False ☐

4. Storm is looking out of the window.

True ☐   False ☐

5. There are three stars decorating the big Christmas tree.

True ☐   False ☐

6. All the presents are under the Christmas tree.

True ☐   False ☐

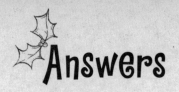

Answers

Snowy Christmas Crossword

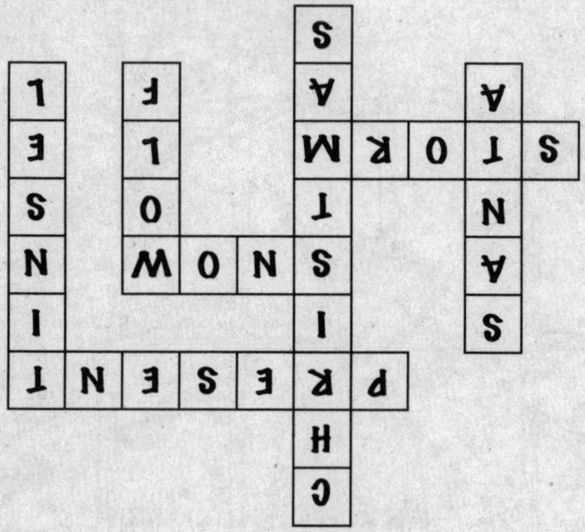

Puppy Trails

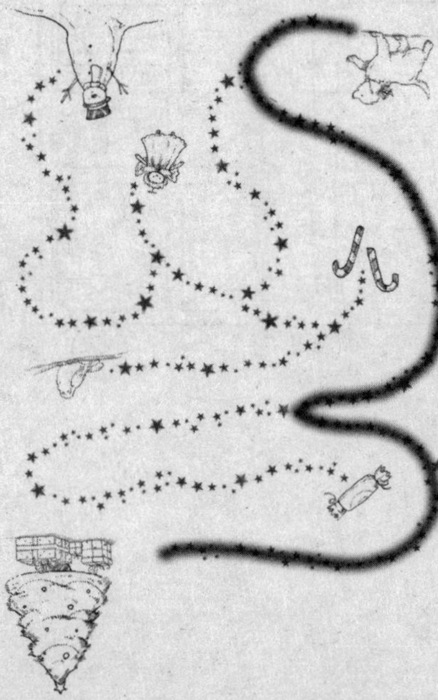

Spot the Difference

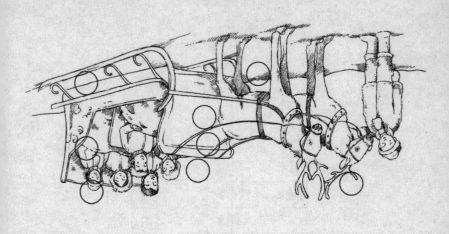

How Many Bones?

There are ten bones in the picture.

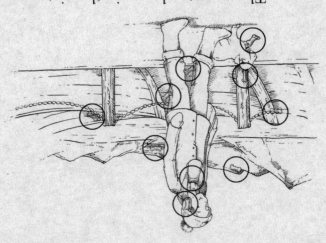

Memory Test

1. False 2. True 3. False 4. False 5. True 6. False

It all started with a Scarecrow.

Puffin is seventy years old.
Sounds ancient, doesn't it? But Puffin has never been
so lively. We're always on the lookout for the next big
idea, which is how it began all those years ago.

Penguin Books was a big idea from the mind of
a man called Allen Lane, who in 1935 invented
the quality paperback and changed the world.
**And from great Penguins, great Puffins grew,
changing the face of children's books forever.**

The first four Puffin Picture Books were hatched in 1940 and the
first Puffin story book featured a man with broomstick arms called
Worzel Gummidge. In 1967 Kaye Webb, Puffin Editor, started the
Puffin Club, promising to **'make children into readers'**.
She kept that promise and over 200,000 children became
devoted Puffineers through their quarterly instalments of
Puffin Post, which is now back for a new generation.

Many years from now, we hope you'll look back and
remember Puffin with a smile. **No matter what your age
or what you're into, there's a Puffin for everyone.**
The possibilities are endless, but one thing is for sure:
whether it's a picture book or a paperback, a sticker book
or a hardback, **if it's got that little Puffin
on it – it's bound to be good.**

Bright and shiny and sizzling with fun stuff . . .

puffin.co.uk

WEB FUN

UNIQUE and exclusive digital content!
Podcasts, photos, Q&A, Day in the Life of, interviews and much more, from Eoin Colfer, Cathy Cassidy, Allan Ahlberg and Meg Rosoff to Lynley Dodd!

WEB NEWS

The **Puffin Blog** is packed with posts and photos from Puffin HQ and special guest bloggers. You can also sign up to our monthly newsletter **Puffin Beak Speak**

WEB CHAT

Discover something new EVERY month – books, competitions and treats galore

WEBBED FEET

(Puffins have funny little feet and brightly coloured beaks)

Point your mouse our way today!